MIGRANT SOULS

Arturo Islas

AVON BOOKS ▲ NEW YORK

AVON BOOKS
A division of
The Hearst Corporation
1350 Avenue of the Americas
New York, New York 10019

Copyright © 1990 by Arturo Islas
Cover art by Terry Widener
Inside cover author photograph by Margo Davis
Published by arrangement with William Morrow and Company, Inc.
Library of Congress Catalog Card Number: 89-13012
ISBN: 0-380-71440-X

First Avon Books Trade Printing: September 1991

AVON TRADEMARK REG. U.S. PAT. OFF. AND IN OTHER COUNTRIES, MARCA REGISTRADA, HECHO EN U.S.A.

Printed in the U.S.A.

OPM   10   9   8   7   6   5   4   3   2

for

my godmother and godfather,
my aunts and cousins,
and my friends

. . . And he took the blind man by the hand and led him out of the village. And when he had spit on his eyes and laid his hands upon him, he asked him, "Do you see anything?" And the blind man looked up and said, "I see men, but they look like trees, walking."

MARK 8:23

BOOK ONE

Flight into Egypt

i

In their mother's eyes, Josie Salazar knew, she and her sister Serena were more like the Indians than the Spanish ladies they were brought up to be.

When they were children and growing up on the "American" side of the Mexican Texas border, it was, "Serena, get that braid out of your mouth. Do you want to be taken for an Indian?" Or, "Josie, how many times do I have to tell you that a young lady does not cross her legs like an Indian?"

Later, when they were teenagers in the late forties and still on the border, Serena was criticized for wearing clothes that were too bright and immodest and Josie was told that if her hair got any stringier because she refused to wash it every day, the Indians were going to claim her as their own and drag her off to Ysleta, or worse yet, to San Elizario, even farther into the lower valley.

Secretly, Josie longed to be dragged by anyone, to

anywhere as long as it was out of her mother's house. "I wonder what life with the Indians is like?" she asked Serena, who remained silent.

Only Ofelia, the eldest of the three sisters, came close to fulfilling their mother Eduviges' dream of producing delicate and tactful young women worthy of their connection to the Angel family name and strong enough to endure the rigorous demands of marriage and motherhood. Even before the age of reason, which the Church had set at seven years old, the girls learned very quickly that their mother's side of the family—the Angel clan—was more important than their father's, the plain old Salazars.

Sancho Salazar, ever wary of large concepts, ignored his relatives altogether and devoted himself to his wife, his daughters and, as often as possible, to hunting and fishing in the mountains and lakes of northern Chihuahua. In that wild country, he told the girls, his Indian blood came to life and made him feel at home with the land and sky. "Don't tell your mother I said these things to you."

Ofelia ignored him when he talked about Mexico. But Serena and Josie sensed that their blood was closer to the earth than an Angel's ought to be. And except for the annual Christmas Eve get-together, they saw that their father made certain he had something else to do whenever his wife reminded him that the Angels were gathering at so-and-so's house to celebrate something or other.

"I am not about to sit through another of those

phony family exercises," Sancho said to Eduviges. "I've got more important things to do. I'm going fishing." And, kissing the girls good-bye after pitching his gear into Serapio Fuentes' beat-up Buick station wagon, he went.

Only Josie did not kiss him back and refused to keep waving along with her sisters until Serapio honked the horn one last time and turned the corner on Cotton Street. Her spirit went with Sancho and she was often thought to be unwell at most Angel family celebrations.

"Are you sick, Josie?" her aunt Mema asked. They were at their great-aunt Cuca's apartment after a baptism party for the girls' cousin JoEl. "Are you missing your daddy?"

Josie looked at her without blinking while Mema felt her forehead and face. She wanted to tell her aunt that they were all lizards shedding their skins in the sun, but just then her grandmother said in Spanish, "Oh, she's all right. She's only being a baby. Always has been. That's what happens to girls who are their father's favorite."

"She'll be all right if you don't tease her," Serena said and put her arm around her sister.

"She's simply acting like an Indian, that's all," their mother said. "Everyone knows they don't talk and can't answer politely when someone asks them a question."

Whispering in her ear, Serena was promising to show Josie the new kittens in Tia Cuca's closet. She knew that if she were not led away, her little sister would remain staring at the older women until they stopped talking about her as if Josie were invisible.

The girls walked quietly down the short hallway into Tia Cuca's bedroom. Shaded by the deep green leaves of the mulberry trees on West Yandell Street, the room was cool and dark and smelled of lavender toilet water.

"Ladies are like flowers," their great-aunt told them often. "They must smell good. Fortunes have been won and lost through the noses of gentlemen." And then, in a velvety voice full of charm, she sang a ditty that always made the girls laugh.

> *Adios, Mama Carlota, narices de pelota,*
> *Adios, Papa Joaquin, narices de violin.*

Josie was not able to understand what a woman with two noses like a ball and a man with two noses like a violin had to do with being a lady.

"It's just a rhyme," Ofelia said, turning up her nose. "It's not supposed to mean anything."

Serena opened the closet door wide and they knelt down in front of a cardboard box lined with old scarves and newspaper. They heard the kittens before they saw them.

"Oh, look!" Serena said. "There are six of them!" She picked up one of the ugly, hairless creatures and put it in the palm of Josie's hand.

"It's hungry, the poor little thing." The high-pitched mewing and blind groping of the animal touched Josie.

"Its dumb mother is over there under the bed," Serena said. "Carlota, come here and feed your babies."

The dirty white she-cat ignored them and went on staring at the floor with demented, ice-blue eyes. "She's acting like they're not hers. I think one of them is dead." Serena shook her head in disapproval.

"Don't worry," Josie said, gently stroking the kitten's back with her little finger. "I'm an Indian. I'll take care of you."

The wind of Del Sapo blew through the trees and the mulberry leaves made a scratching noise against the window panes. Five centuries earlier, the Spanish explorers had named the region for the craggy mountain range around which the town grew. To them, it had looked like a squatting toad.

Josie and Serena peered out at Del Sapo Mountain from Tia Cuca's bedroom and watched the late afternoon clouds make shadow figures that flew like ghosts on its dry, rocky surface. The slanting light from the west was shifting in color from brown slate to rose. Josie yawned.

"I don't think the mountain looks like a horny toad," Serena said.

"I do. Tia Cuca lives under its right eye," Josie said. "Our house is near its nose. Mama Chona told me. Look, Serena, a fish cloud!"

Serena saw only the wind blowing the desert into

Del Sapo. The smell of dust in the room was now stronger than the lavender. She took the kitten from Josie and put it back in the closet.

"Come on. We better go back. Mom will want us to get home before the dust storm gets real bad."

Hand in hand, they walked into Tia Cuca's parlor. The wind made siren noises through the hall windows. Their mother and the two old ladies were sipping the last of the *manzanilla* tea they drank for arthritis.

"There you are, girls," Mama Chona said to them in Spanish and smiled. "Have you been saying your afternoon prayers?"

ii

The girls' only surviving grandparent—Encarnacion Olmeca, or Mama Chona as she instructed them to call her—may have had the Indian origins her maiden name suggested, but she had married Jesus Angel. By this act, as well as by her baptism into the Church of Rome, Mama Chona felt herself and her children to have been elevated into civilization for all time.

It was assumed and later accepted by the family—why should they argue with myth?—that Jesus Angel had more Spanish than Indian blood in his

8

veins. And, the legend continued, if his ancestors had not been in the first army of *conquistadores,* they certainly had sailed in shortly thereafter. With an eternal sense of purpose and a determination peculiar to their name, Mama Chona told her grandchildren, the Angels discovered and claimed their portion of Mexico after surveying it with pure Castilian and Catholic eyes.

Josie was five years old the first time she heard about her grandfather. Jesus Angel's large, clear eyes looked out and down at her from an enlarged, hazy photograph Mama Chona had plucked out of the flames in the early years of the Mexican Revolution when the family was forced to flee northward to Texas. If the photograph was to be trusted, Jesus Angel was a very fair-skinned man, handsome and in his mid-forties. Josie was fascinated by the perfectly trimmed moustache and a forehead so high and wide it all but faded into the background. For ethereal purposes, Mama Chona had chosen an oval-shaped mahogany frame with a convex glass for it which created a bulging effect that gave Josie and some of her cousins the creeps.

It was part of the young Angels' education to be introduced to the photograph during a ceremony of hot chocolate and sweet bread made the Mexican way. Mama Chona spoke about their grandfather's qualities and accomplishments as if he were a divine presence in the room and not simply a picture on the wall of her small, dusty-smelling parlor. Because she had lived so many years without him in the flesh, every word she said about him made Jesus Angel larger than life.

"Jesus Angel was a very great man," she told them. "Kind, honest, and absolutely devoted to his family." When she said his name, Mama Chona waited a few moments for the children to be impressed by all the celestial reverberations it was meant to produce.

In that period, their grandmother was living in a one-bedroom house built for her and her adopted son Ricardo by the contributions and labor of her six surviving children. The *casita* was in the Five Points area of the border town and not far from the *barrio* where the family had first settled decades earlier.

Wherever she lived, Mama Chona was careful to create an otherworldly atmosphere by paying little attention to the concrete arrangement of furniture and by focusing only on those sacred objects that bound her and her family to the Angel traditions: an enormous and worn wooden chest, its leather straps frayed and hanging useless front and back, which she told them contained the documents and relics that proved that the Angels had descended from castles in Spain; a very chipped statue of Jesus, almost twenty inches high, the right index finger repaired and pointing to His Sacred Heart; and the imposingly framed photograph of her husband.

Staring at it while she and her sisters were waiting for Mama Chona to bring them more hot chocolate on that cold, early Spring day before Easter, Josie was amazed by the deceased patriarch's high and wide forehead. Her mother had finally relented and allowed her to attend the ceremony with her older sisters, though Eduviges continued to insist up to the last minute that Josie was still too young to grasp the full meaning of the ritual of introduction.

"Oh, let her go," Sancho said. "Josie's old enough to start finding out how crazy your family is, Vickie. The sooner she knows, the sooner she can adjust."

"My family is not crazy," Eduviges said in what the girls called her dangerous tone.

Sancho ignored her. He was helping his daughters into the old Chevy he had fixed up again and again. The children called it the band-aid car. Before his wife could stop him, he grabbed Josie, tossed her into the air, and then into the backseat. On her way down, Josie caught a glimpse of the top of her mother's head and the bulge of her brow.

...
iii

The desert light in Mama Chona's parlor was very bright, and the patches of sun on the rose-colored carpet sent the brightness straight into the air and gave the photograph an eerie sheen. Josie was sitting directly across the room from it.

"He was a gnome," she said out loud. In her mouth, the word was two syllables and the "g" was very hard.

"Be quiet," Ofelia said, brushing invisible crumbs from her lap. She loved clothes and especially the light green dress she was wearing. Her mother had embroidered the flowers on the sleeves. "Mama Chona will hear you."

"I don't care," Josie said. "He looks like a gnome."

Serena, sitting with her knees apart while their grandmother was out of the room, giggled. Silently, she agreed with her baby sister. Her dress was a faded cinnamon brown color and made her seem nunnish to Josie. No embroidery decorated its sleeves, she noticed.

"What did you say, Josefa?" Mama Chona asked, floating into the room on a cloud of chocolate and old age smells.

Naming her Josefa was the first crime Josie felt her mother had committed against her. Hearing it spoken by Mama Chona—she never used diminutives, only uneducated, impolite people used them— reminded her that she had been born on the feast of Saint Joseph, for Mama Chona said all of her children's and grandchildren's names as if addressing their patron saints and not them.

Seeing that Josie was about to repeat what she had said, Serena quickly put a piece of sweet bread in her sister's mouth. "Josie, I mean Josefa, said how noble Grandfather looks, Mama Chona." She offered a piece of sweet bread to her older sister. "Isn't that right, Ofelia?"

"Yes," Ofelia said. She knew that of the three, she was Mama Chona's favorite. "Isn't it wonderful how little Josefa has learned to use such words? I can't imagine that she understands them yet. This bread is delicious, Mama Chona."

Josie swallowed and said, "I didn't say that at all. I said Grandfather looks like a gnome."

"Don't say 'guh-nome,' Josefa. It's just 'nome' as if the 'g' wasn't there." By correcting her little sister, Ofelia was hoping to deflect their grandmother's displeasure. Mama Chona wanted her to be a schoolteacher when she grew up.

Before Josie could tell Ofelia she would talk any way she felt like talking, Mama Chona surprised them all by laughing and saying, "Do you really think so, Josefa? Well, in a way, I suppose he was."

And then, in that high-pitched voice that bored and hypnotized her grandchildren, she went on to tell them in what ways gnomes were related to angels. Moving her chair closer to Mama Chona, Ofelia, sincerely interested, asked her to tell them more about such heavenly relations. She believed it when their mother's mother told them that gnomes guarded the treasures inside the earth just as the angels stood watch over the treasures of heaven.

"You see, children, our Father created the highest and the lowliest of creatures. Good men like your

Grandfather—may he rest in peace in the blessed arms of our Lord Jesus—are very close to the angels. And you must try to be as much like them as possible."

She was speaking to them in a Spanish learned from nuns during her early years of convent school in San Miguel de Allende. When she lapsed into English, she cautioned the girls not to imitate her accent but instead to listen carefully to their Anglo schoolteachers. Though she understood that God was omnipotent, in her heart Mama Chona felt He spoke to her only in Spanish.

At the end of the morning's instruction on the angels, Mama Chona said, "It's more difficult for girls to be like angels because they are born wicked in a different way from boys."

She stroked Ofelia's forehead and smiled at Serena and Josie from her place beneath the sacred picture on the wall. At that moment a cloud passed between them and the sun and the room darkened. Josie felt their grandmother had arranged for the sky to do her bidding so that they would believe her every word.

Ofelia was old enough to sense that the difference in the wickedness of boys and girls had something to do with "down there" and drank in every phrase with each sip of the hot chocolate. The cloud in the room only made her feel more convinced of the order in the universe Mama Chona taught them was divine.

Half listening, Serena was more interested in watching the movement of the dust motes in the sun squares that began floating along the carpet toward and out of the windows after the cloud had passed. She could not understand how the specks moved and stood still at the same time. They made her sleepy and she stifled a yawn. Their grandmother frowned on yawning as not ladylike. It was almost noon.

Josie, chewing on her tongue, was thinking that she would be much happier as a gnome pronounced her way and fought against believing what Mama Chona was saying to them about girls. She was growing very tired of the old woman's voice and did not like the daffy look on Ofelia's face. Looking away from them, she saw that Serena was just about to fall out of her chair.

Josie felt a great longing for their earthly father to come for them and take them home. The chocolate and sweetbread were stones in her belly and the dress her mother had made her wear was tightening around her chest and throat. A knock at the door saved her from choking.

"That's your father," Mama Chona said in a tone that dismissed as inferior all of her children's wives and husbands. "He's late, as usual. Never mind. He's given me more time with you girls."

Before opening the door, she told them not to forget what they had talked about and to pray for the soul of their grandfather. The sun brightened the room once again, and Josie felt she was being allowed into a secret room that Mama Chona prepared for a special and privileged few.

"We won't forget, Mama Chona," Ofelia said, imitating their grandmother's perfectly polite and insincere tone.

Josie wanted to tell her sister to speak for herself, but was so happy to see her father's shiny face at the door that she kept her mouth shut. He was in his work clothes and kept wiping his brow with a soiled handkerchief.

"Won't you come in, Sancho?" Mama Chona asked him. She was offended by his soiled appearance and remained on her side of the screen door.

"No, Señora Angel. Thank you very much." He alone in the family did not call her Mama Chona and spoke to her with great courtesy as if he were her servant. "I have to get back to the station. I left Eduviges there all by herself. You know how it is on Saturdays. Are you ready, girls?"

He stayed outside the door. His beat-up coffee-colored hat in hand, Sancho waited for them to say good-bye to his mother-in-law.

"Tell Eduviges that I want to see her," she said to him. "I look forward to your next visit, girls. Remember what I told you."

An enormous white cloud cast them into the shadows and turned them into figures that looked like the photo negatives Josie had seen for the first time that week. She grabbed for her father's hand.

"Well, how was your visit to the other world,

girls? How many angels did she tell you danced on the head of a pin?" His voice made Josie breathe more easily.

Ofelia and Serena told him about the chocolate and sweet bread. Josie said nothing. The stories about her grandfather sounded fishy to her, but she did wonder how Mama Chona made the sun and clouds obey her.

iv

When they were not visiting Mama Chona, Eduviges took her children to Juarez on Saturdays. Food at the markets there, especially meat, was much cheaper than at the local Piggly Wiggly on the American side, and Eduviges could save on ration stamps.

The girls loved these "smuggling" trips during the war. They knew it was illegal to bring meat and other foods across the border from Mexico. But Eduviges, and many mothers like her north of the river, ignored the law and, from the money they saved, were able to feed meat to their children once a week. Later, in her teens, Josie realized that such a luxury made her and her family hopelessly middle class, even if in the lower part of it. From the start, she loved putting catsup on chicken-fried steak.

Each marketing day, the girls put on their newest

pair of shoes and dressed in their best outfits. Pink or rose for Ofelia, blue or brown for Serena, and whatever hand-me-down color looked the least worn for Josie. Their hair was braided tightly and wound above their foreheads like coronets. Ofelia's hair, a thick dark caramel, divided into braids that circled twice in both directions. Serena and Josie had less brilliant and much shorter hair, and that was why, Josie concluded, they were not given the privilege of sitting in the front seat with their mother.

"It's not fair," Josie said. "Of course, Ofelia has more hair. She's lived longer than us. I think we should take turns sitting in the front seat."

"It's not because of her hair, Josie," Eduviges said. "It's because she is the oldest and can help me if anything goes wrong, God forbid." Their mother was always ready for disaster. "Please try to understand and don't bother me about it anymore."

"We'll never get to sit in front, then. It's just not fair," Josie said logically and into the void.

Serena, who wanted to cut off her braids and have hair as short as a boy's, winked and whispered that the two of them could play a special, secret game in the back seat that would leave out Ofelia and their unfair mother. She made a funny face toward the front seat which Josie ignored.

"I don't want to play any secret game," she said loudly enough for her mother to hear. "I want to sit up front."

"Come on, baby. Play a game with me." Serena pinched her in a ticklish way.

"Stop it," Josie said.

"I won't till you stop sulking. I can't stand it when you look like that."

"I don't care." Josie concentrated on keeping her face as hard as she could, even if it ached.

"Think of all the starving children in the world." Serena knew her little sister's weaknesses.

"Stop it!" In spite of herself, Josie's face softened.

"That's better," Serena said. "Now, let's play 'Michelle, mew-mew-mew.' " This game began with a gentle caress of the cheeks while saying "Michelle" and ended with five sharp slaps that made their faces red. The trick was not knowing when the other person was going to say "mew-mew-mew" and start slapping. With great delight, the girls had invented the game after watching the way their friend Colette played with Michelle, her fat and gorgeous silver-blue cat.

"Okay," Josie said. "But don't cry if I slap you too hard. Promise?"

Serena promised. But after the second round, she was unable to hold back the tears of laughter and began hooting with pleasure.

"Girls," Eduviges said crossly. "I've told you not to play that silly game. You're going to poke each other's eyes out. The two of you are going to drive me crazy."

Josie and Serena looked at each other and laughed into their hands.

V

After the war, their mother took to raising chickens and pigeons in order to save money. Josie saw their neighbors enjoying life and thought that her mother had gone crazy. Eduviges had even bought a live duck from God knows where and kept it until the Garcias next door began complaining about all the racket it made at night. Josie and Serena had become attached to it, so much so that when it appeared piecemeal in a *mole poblano,* both of them refused to eat it.

"It's too greasy," Josie said, holding back her tears and criticizing her mother's cooking instead.

"Then let your sisters have your portion. Eat the beans," Sancho said from behind the hunting magazine that was his bible.

"I don't want it," Serena said, her tears falling unchecked. "Poor don Pato. He didn't make that much noise. The Garcias are louder than he ever was."

Ofelia was dutifully, even happily, chewing away. "I think he's delicious," she said.

Josie glared at her and held her hands tightly under the table and away from the knife next to her plate. In her mind, she was dumping its contents into Ofelia's lap.

Eduviges stared at her husband until the silence made him glance up from his magazine. "Well," she said, "if your little darlings won't eat what I raise, slaughter, and cook with my own hands, let them live on beans. I know Josie likes chicken well enough. And pigeon stew. From now on, she can do the killing before she eats them. Let's see how she likes it."

And then speaking to Josie directly, she added, "This is not a restaurant, young lady. You have to eat what I serve you. And that's that." She said nothing to Serena, who was blowing her nose loudly into a paper napkin and not glaring at her in an accusing way.

"Leave her alone," Sancho said, meaning Josie. "The child liked that dumb duck, that's all. She doesn't have to eat him if she doesn't want to." These words caused Josie to leave the table in tears, followed by Serena, now struck by another fit of weeping. Ofelia kept eating and asked that her sisters' portions be passed to her.

"Of course, darling," Eduviges said. Sancho returned to his magazine.

In their bedroom, Josie and Serena held each other until they stopped crying. "I'll never forgive her for killing him," Josie said.

"Oh, Josie, don't say that. I was crying because of the way you were looking at Ofelia and Mother. We can always get another duck."

After don Pato's transformation, their mother stuck to chickens and pigeons. Atoning for her harshness toward Josie, she cooked omelets and looked the other way whenever Serena slipped Josie a piece of chicken. But for Thanksgiving in 1947, Eduviges, in a fit of guilt, decided to bake a turkey with all the trimmings. She had memorized the recipes in the glossy American magazines while waiting her turn at the Safeway checkout counter.

Because the girls were in public school and learning about North American holidays and customs, Eduviges thought her plan would please them. It did and even Josie allowed her mother to embrace her in that quick, embarrassed way she had of touching them. As usual, Sancho had no idea why she was going to such lengths preparing for a ritual that meant nothing to him.

"I don't see why we can't have the enchiladas you always make," he said. "I don't even like turkey. Why don't you let me bring you a nice, fat pheasant from the Chihuahua mountains? At least it'll taste like something. Eating turkey is going to turn my girls into little *gringas*. Is that what you want?"

"Oh, Daddy, please! Everybody else is going to have turkey." The girls, wearing colored paper headdresses they had made in art class, were acting out the Pocahontas story and reciting from "Hiawatha" in a hodgepodge of Indian sentiment that forced Sancho to agree in order to keep them quiet.

"All right, all right," he said. "Just stop all the racket, please. And Serena, *querida*, don't wear that stuff outside the house or they'll pick you up and send you to a reservation. That would be okay with me, but your mother wouldn't like it."

Serena and Josie gave each other knowing glances. "They" were the *migra,* who drove around in their green vans, sneaked up on innocent dark-skinned people, and deported them. Their neighbor down the block—Benito Cruz, who was lighter-skinned than Serena and did not look at all like an Indian—had been picked up three times already, detained at the border for hours, and then released with the warning that he was to carry his identification papers at all times. That he was an American citizen did not seem to matter to the immigration officers.

The Angel children were brought up on as many deportation stories as fairy tales and family legends. The latest border incident had been the discovery of twenty-one young Mexican males who had been left to asphyxiate in an airtight boxcar on their way to pick cotton in the lower Rio Grande Valley.

When they read the newspaper articles about how the men died, both Josie and Serena thought of the fluttering noises made by the pigeons their mother first strangled and then put under a heavy cardboard box for minutes that seemed eternal to the girls. They covered their ears to protect their souls from the thumping and scratching noises of the doomed birds.

Even their mother had shown sympathy for the Mexican youths, especially when it was learned that they were not from the poorest class. "I feel very bad for their families," she said. "Their mothers must be in agony."

What about their fathers? Josie felt like asking but did not. Because of the horror she imagined they went through, Josie did not want to turn her own feelings for the young men into yet another argument with her mother about "wetbacks" or about who did and did not "deserve" to be in the United States.

In the first semester of seventh grade, Josie had begun to wonder why being make-believe North American Indians seemed to be all right with their mother. "Maybe it was because those Indians spoke English," Josie said to Serena. Mexican Indians were too close to home and the truth, and the way Eduviges looked at Serena in her art class getup convinced Josie she was on the right track.

That year on the Saturday before Thanksgiving, their mother and father took them across the river in search of the perfect turkey. Sancho borrowed his friend Tacho Morales' pickup and they drove down the valley to the Zaragoza crossing. It was closer to the ranch where Eduviges had been told the turkeys were raised and sold for practically nothing. Josie and Serena sat in the front seat of the pickup with their father. Eduviges and Ofelia followed them in the Chevy in case anything went wrong.

Sancho was a slower, more patient driver than their mother, who turned into a speed demon with a sharp tongue behind the wheel. More refined than her younger sisters, Ofelia was scandalized by every phrase that came out of Eduviges' mouth when some sorry driver from Chihuahua or New Mexico got in her way.

"Why don't they teach those imbecilic cretins how to drive?" she said loudly in Spanish, window down and honking. Or, "May all your teeth fall out but one and may that ache until the day you die" to the man who pulled out in front of her without a signal.

Grateful that her mother was being good for once and following slowly and at a safe distance behind the pickup, Ofelia dozed, barely aware of the clear day so warm for November. Only the bright yellow leaves of the cottonwood trees reminded her that it was autumn. They clung to the branches and vibrated in the breeze, which smelled of burning mesquite and Mexican alders. As they followed her father away from the mountains and into the valley, Ofelia began to dream they were inside one of Mama Chona's Mexican blue clay bowls, suspended in midair while the sky revolved around them.

To Josie and Serena, it seemed their father was taking forever to get to where they were going. "Are we there yet?" they asked him until he told them that if they asked again, he would leave them in the middle of nowhere and not let their mother rescue them. The threat only made them laugh more and they started asking him where the middle of nowhere was until he, too, laughed with them.

"The middle of nowhere, smart alecks, is at the bottom of the sea and so deep not even the fish go there," Sancho said, getting serious about it.

"No, no," Serena said. "It's in the space between two stars and no planets around."

"I already said the middle of nowhere is in Del Sapo, Texas," Josie said, not wanting to get serious.

"I know, I know. It's in the Sahara Desert where not even the tumbleweeds will grow," their father said.

"No, Daddy. It's at the top of Mount Everest." Serena was proud of the B she had gotten for her report on the highest mountain in the world. They fell silent and waited for Josie to take her turn.

"It's here," Josie said quietly and pointed to her heart.

"Oh, for heaven's sake, Josie, don't be so dramatic. You don't even know what you are saying," Serena said. Their father changed the subject.

When they arrived at the ranch, he told Eduviges and the girls that the worst that could happen on their return was that the turkey would be taken away from them. But the girls, especially, must do and say exactly as he instructed them.

Their mother was not satisfied with Sancho's simple directions and once again told them about the humiliating body search her friend from New Mexico, *la señora* Moulton, had been subjected to at the Santa Fe Street bridge. She had just treated her daughter Ethel and her granddaughters, Amy and

Mary Ann, to lunch at the old Central Cafe in Juarez. When *la señora* had been asked her citizenship, she had replied in a jovial way, "Well, what do I look like, sir?"

They made her get out of the car, led her to a special examining cell, ordered her to undress, and made her suffer unspeakable mortifications while her relatives waited at least four hours in terror, wondering if they would ever see her again or be allowed to return to the country of their birth. Then, right on cue, Josie and Serena said along with Eduviges, "And they were Anglos and blond!"

While their parents were bargaining for the bird, the girls looked with awe upon the hundreds of adult turkeys kept inside four large corrals. As they walked by each enclosure, one of the birds gobbled and the rest echoed its call until the racket was unbearable. Serena was struck by an attack of giggles.

"They sure are stupid," Josie said in Spanish to their Mexican guide.

"They really are," he said with a smile. "When it rains, we have to cover the coops of the younger ones so they won't drown." He was a dark red color and very shy. Josie liked him instantly.

"How can they drown?" Serena asked him. "The river is nowhere near here. Does it flood?"

"No," the young man said, looking away from them. "Not from the Rio Bravo. From the rain itself. They stretch their necks, open their beaks wide, and let it pour in until they drown. They keel over all bloated. That's how stupid they are." He bent his head back and showed them as they walked by an enclosure. "Gobble, gobble," the guide called and the turkeys answered hysterically.

Josie and Serena laughed all the way back to the pickup. Ofelia had not been allowed to join them because of the way their mother thought the guide was looking at her. She was dreaming away in the backseat of the Chevy while their father struggled to get the newly bought and nervous turkey into a slatted crate. Eduviges was criticizing every move he made. At last, the creature was in the box and eerily silent.

"Now remember, girls," Sancho said, wiping his face, "I'll do all the talking at the bridge. You just say 'American' when the time comes. Not another word, you hear? Think about Mrs. Moulton, Josie." He gave her a wink.

The turkey remained frozen inside the crate. Sancho lifted it onto the pickup, covered it with a yellow plastic tablecloth they used on picnics, and told Serena to sit on top of it with her back against the rear window.

"Serena," he said, "I'd hate to lose you because of this stupid bird, but if you open your mouth except to say 'American,' I won't be responsible for what happens. Okay?" He kissed her on the cheek as if in farewell forever, Josie thought, looking at them from the front seat. She was beginning to wish they had not begged so successfully for a traditional

North American ceremony. Nothing would happen to Ofelia, of course. She was protected in their mother's car and nowhere near the turkey. Josie felt that Serena was in great peril and made up her mind to do anything to keep her from harm.

On the way to the bridge, Josie made the mistake of asking her father if they were aliens. Sancho put his foot on the brake so hard that Eduviges almost rear-ended the truck. He looked at Josie very hard and said, "I do not ever want to hear you use that word in my presence again. About anybody. We are not aliens. We are American citizens of Mexican heritage. We are proud of both countries and have never and will never be that word you just said to me."

"Well," Josie said. Sancho knew she was not afraid of him. He pulled the truck away from the shoulder and signaled for his wife to continue following them. "That's what they call Mexican people in all the newspapers. And Kathy Jarvis at school told me real snotty at recess yesterday that we were nothing but a bunch of resident aliens."

After making sure Eduviges was right behind them, Sancho said in a calmer, serious tone, "Josie, I'm warning you. I do not want to hear those words again. Do you understand me?"

"I'm only telling you what Kathy told me. What did she mean? Is she right?"

"Kathy Jarvis is an ignorant little brat. The next time she tells you that, you tell her that Mexican and Indian people were in this part of the country long before any *gringos,* Europeans (he said 'Yurrup-beans') or anyone else decided it was theirs. That should shut her up. If it doesn't, tell her those words are used by people who think Mexicans are not human beings. That goes for the newspapers, too. They don't think anyone is human." She watched him look straight ahead, then in the rearview mirror, then at her as he spoke.

"Don't you see, Josie. When people call Mexicans those words, it makes it easier for them to deport or kill them. Aliens come from outer space." He paused. "Sort of like your mother's family, the blessed Angels, who think they come from heaven. Don't tell her I said that."

Before he made that last comment, Josie was impressed by her father's tone. Sancho seldom became that passionate in their presence about any issue. He laughed at the serious and the pompous and especially at religious fanatics.

During their aunt Jesus Maria's visits, the girls and their cousins were sent out of the house in the summer or to the farthest room away from the kitchen in the winter so that they would not be able to hear her and Sancho arguing about God and the Church. Unnoticed, the children sneaked around the house and crouched in the honeysuckle under the kitchen window, wide open to the heat of July. In horror and amusement, they listened to Jesus Maria tell Sancho that he would burn in hell for all eternity because he did not believe in an afterlife and dared to criticize the infallibility of the Pope.

"It's because they're afraid of dying that people make up an afterlife to believe in," Sancho said.

"That's not true. God created Heaven, Hell, and Purgatory before He created man. And you are going to end up in Hell if you don't start believing what the Church teaches us." Jesus Maria was in her glory defending the teachings of Roman Catholicism purged by the fires of the Spanish Inquisition.

"Oh, Jessie—" he began.

"Don't call me that. My name is Jesus Maria and I am proud of it." She knew the children were listening.

"Excuse me, Jesus Maria," he said with a flourish. "I just want to point out to you that it's hotter here in Del Sapo right now than in hell." He saw her bristle but went on anyway. "Haven't you figured it out yet? This is hell and heaven and purgatory right here. How much worse, better, or boring can the afterlife be?" Sancho was laughing at his own insight.

"If you are going to start joking about life-and-death matters, I simply won't talk about anything serious with you again," their aunt said. They knew she meant it. "I, like the Pope, am fighting for your everlasting soul, Sancho. If I did not love you because you are my sister's husband, I would not be telling you these things."

"Thank you, Jessie. I appreciate your efforts and love. But the Pope is only a man. He is not Christ.

Don't you read history? All most popes have cared about is money and keeping the poor in rags so that they can mince about in gold lamé dresses."

"Apostate!" their aunt cried.

"What's that?" Serena whispered to Josie.

"I don't know but it sounds terrible. We'll look it up in the dictionary as soon as they stop." They knew the arguing was almost over when their aunt began calling their father names. Overwhelmed by the smell of the honeysuckle, the children ran off to play kick the can. Later, when Josie looked up the word "apostate," she kept its meaning to herself because she knew that Serena believed in an afterlife and would be afraid for her father.

That one word affected her father more than another was a mystery to Josie. She loved words and believed them to be more real than whatever they described. In her mind, she, too, suspected that she was an apostate but, like her father, she did not want to be an alien.

"All right, Daddy. I promise I won't say that word again. And I won't tell Mother what you said about the Angels."

They were now driving through the main streets of Juarez, and Sancho was fighting to stay in his lane. "God, these Mexicans drive like your mother," he said with affection.

At every intersection, young Indian women with babies at their breast stretched out their hands. Josie was filled with dread and pity. One of the women knocked on her window while they waited for the light to change. She held up her baby and said, *"Señorita, por favor. Dinero para el niño."* Her hair was black and shiny and her eyes as dark as Josie's. The words came through the glass in a muted, dreamlike way. Silent and unblinking, the infant stared at Josie. She had a quarter in her pocket.

"Don't roll down the window or your mother will have a fit," Sancho said. He turned the corner and headed toward the river. The woman and child disappeared. Behind them, Eduviges kept honking almost all the way to the bridge.

"I think it was blind," Josie said. Her father did not answer and looked straight ahead.

The traffic leading to the declaration points was backed up several blocks, and the stop-and-go movement as they inched their way to the American side was more than Josie could bear. She kept looking back at Serena, who sat like a *Virgen de Guadalupe* statue on her yellow plastic-covered throne.

Knowing her sister, Josie was certain that Serena was going to free the turkey, jump out of the truck with it, gather up the beggarly women and children, and disappear forever into the sidestreets and alleys of Juarez. They drove past an old Indian woman, her long braids silver gray in the sun, begging in front of Curley's Club. And that is how Josie imagined Serena years from that day—an ancient and withered creature, bare feet crusted with clay, too old to recognize her little sister. The vision made her believe that the middle of nowhere was exactly where she felt it was. She covered her chest with her arms.

"What's the matter? Don't tell me you're going to be sick," her father said.

"No. I'm fine. Can't you hurry?"

Seeing the fear in her face, Sancho told her gently that he had not yet figured out how to drive through cars without banging them up. Josie smiled and kept her hands over her heart.

When they approached the border patrolman's station, the turkey began gobbling away. "Oh, no," Josie cried and shut her eyes in terror for her sister.

"Oh, shit," her father said. "I hate this god-damned bridge." At that moment, the officer stuck his head into the pickup and asked for their citizenship.

"American," said Sancho.

"American," said Josie.

"Anything to declare? Any liquor or food?" he asked in an accusing way. While Sancho was assuring him that there was nothing to declare, the turkey gobbled again in a long stream of high-pitched gurgles that sent shivers up and down Josie's spine. She vowed to go into the cell with Serena when the search was ordered.

"What's that noise?" the patrolman wanted to know. Sancho shrugged and gave Josie and then the officer a look filled with the ignorance of the world.

Behind them, Serena began gobbling along with the bird and it was hard for them to tell one gobble from another. Their mother pressed down on the horn of the Chevy and made it stick. Eduviges was ready to jump out of the car and save her daughter from a fate worse than death. In the middle of the racket, the officer's frown was turning into anger and he started yelling at Serena.

"American!" she yelled back and gobbled.

"What have you got there?" The officer pointed to the plastic-covered crate.

"It's a turkey," Serena shouted. "It's American, too." She kept gobbling along with the noise of the horn. Other drivers had begun honking with impatience.

The patrolman looked at her and yelled, "Sure it is! Don't move," he shouted toward Sancho.

Eduviges had opened the hood and was pretending not to know what to do. Rushing toward the officer, she grabbed him by the sleeve and pulled him away from the pickup. Confused by the din, he made gestures that Sancho took as permission to drive away. "Relax, *señora*. Please let go of my arm."

In the truck, Sancho was laughing like a maniac and wiping the tears and his nose on his sleeve. "Look at that, Josie. The guy is twice as big as your mother."

She was too scared to laugh and did not want to look. Several blocks into South Del Sapo, she was still trembling. Serena kept on gobbling in case they were being followed by the *migra* in unmarked cars.

Fifteen minutes later, Eduviges and Ofelia caught

up with them on Alameda Street. Sancho signaled his wife to follow him into the vacant lot next to Don Luis Leal's Famous Tex-Mex Diner. They left the turkey unattended and silent once more.

"Dumb bird," Sancho said. With great ceremony, he treated them to *menudo* and *gorditas* washed down with as much Coca-Cola as they could drink.

vi

Eduviges was hardly aware of the odds against such a purely Spanish upbringing for the children yet to come when, along with her brothers and sisters and mother, she found herself crossing the border between Mexico and the United States in the second decade of the twentieth century. Her father, Jesus Angel, had died or been killed, they did not yet know which, and in that journey northward, Mama Chona gave birth to her last child, a son she named Miguel in a fit of nostalgia for her firstborn. Eduviges was ten years old.

Eduviges Maria was a small child with dark eyes, a prominent brow, and cheekbones she learned to powder later on in life so that she might appear as light-skinned as her sisters Jesus Maria and Eufemia Maria. Mama Chona seemed to pay little attention to her middle daughter, who obeyed her wishes silently and as if gliding through a dream of life.

Only occasionally did Eduviges display her true
nature in flashes of temper she quickly disguised so
as not to appear willful, especially in her mother's
presence. Daily, she practiced hiding her will, more
bronze than iron, behind a mask of shyness that led
others to notice her older and younger sisters before
they became aware of the quiet, docile child standing
behind her mother's chair. By then, Eduviges had
sized up the visitors and found them wanting.

Mama Chona was not fooled. She sensed Eduviges' strength and cultivated it in a seemingly indifferent but careful manner. She saw to it that
Eduviges learned about the slaughtering of animals
on their ranch in Chihuahua. From the beginning,
Eduviges was a willing pupil and, ignoring the
wretched squeals of the pigs, stood by the dying
animals for as long as it took their blood to seep into
the dry earth.

Later, watching Eduviges eat the slice of roasted
pork on her plate with relish, Mama Chona saw that
this child was able to separate what she saw from
what she ate. Jesus Maria and Eufemia Maria, Mama
Chona knew, were two sides of the same coin—the
spiritual and the sensual—and she predicted cor-
rectly that their lives would be filled with misery and
heartache. Only Eduviges seemed destined to enjoy
some measure of worldly happiness.

"Aren't you sorry for the poor pig, Eduviges?"
Mama Chona felt it her duty to test her children's
strength.

"No, Mama," Eduviges replied. "Should I be?"

And she asked if she could have a second helping.

Making their way through the dusty streets of Del Sapo on a hot and windy afternoon in August, Eduviges and her brothers and sisters, trying hard to ignore their empty stomachs, had to squint to keep the sand out of their eyes and on the back of Jesus Maria's head. As the oldest surviving child, Jesus Maria walked beside Mama Chona, ready to relieve her of the infant in her arms. For now, as they made their way from one country to another, eyes straight ahead, avoiding the gutters running red with the blood of the dead and wounded lying in the streets of Juarez and indifferent to the brown ooze of the river under the bridge, Jesus Maria's long and thick dark brown hair, tied at the shoulders with a white ribbon and falling to her waist, was their only flag.

Their mother hated flags and from the start had looked with scorn on the Revolution that drove them away from their home. "It's just another excuse for the men to kill each other and make everyone miserable," Mama Chona said for all to hear.

The reports that had reached them from the capital were contradictory and colored by the bias of the messengers. "Zapata has entered Mexico City. Porfirio Diaz has been assassinated. Madero is now in command and has the support of the country. Zapata is dead. Pancho Villa sits triumphantly in Diaz' chair."

Mama Chona believed none of these outrages and devoted herself to her duties as wife, mother, and mistress of a modest but productive ranch. By then, she had grown to love the bleak desert landscape and no longer missed the fragrance of the flowers in San Miguel de Allende, the place of her birth.

"I don't know what they think they're doing except ruining this country with their greed and lust after power," Mama Chona said to Eva Soriano, the cleaning lady. "Revolution! I don't see that they are changing human beings into loving creatures."

"Si, señora," Eva responded. She was a follower of Pancho Villa and had grown tired of the way the central government ignored the Northern Provinces. Secretly, silently, she considered her mistress a snob and the sort of idealist who would be good to her as long as she stayed in her place.

"There has only been one real revolution in the history of this dismal world," Mama Chona said and believed. "They nailed Him to a cross."

"Si, señora," Eva said and went on with the dusting. In her eyes, the Church was one more way to keep poor people ignorant and hungry. No priest had ever helped her feed her children.

"Don't forget to look carefully into the ceiling corners, Eva. I found cobwebs and spider mites there after you were here last time. I know it's not your fault. They spring up overnight."

"No, señora. I won't forget." Eva instantly walked toward the nearest corner and reached as high as she could with the feather duster.

Mama Chona ignored Eva's insolent ways because she had proved herself a good and dependable servant. She was not like Marta the cook, who refused to allow her mistress into the kitchen except when one of the children broke a pot or stole tastes from the pan and ruined her *flan.* Mama Chona had dismissed Placencia the nanny for slapping her son Felix. Beyond her front and back yards, Jesus took care of the ranch hands. They came and went with the Revolution.

"Well, they are not going to accomplish anything except the destruction of Mexico. If they don't stop, we are all going to be forced to talk like the North Americans." The Revolution was in its fifth year.

That morning Eva, ever devoted and on time, pretended not to hear *la señora*'s remarks and walked out of the room without excusing herself. She was looking for the broom.

Eva knew that her mistress judged her ignorant because of the way she spoke Spanish. She smiled when she imagined herself speaking in English. Rifles speak louder than words, she thought.

The broom was in the hallway and she began sweeping the tile floor in the entryway. That afternoon before paying her, Mama Chona insisted she get on her hands and knees and wash it with vinegar water.

Even after she lost her beloved, the first Miguel and her oldest child, Mama Chona still refused to take sides in the daily violent struggles around her.

When they transported her son's body from San Miguel to the ranch, she did not ask which camp fired the bullet that killed him. He was seventeen and in his first year at the university.

She prepared him for burial and did not let anyone else touch him. "You promised you would return to me safely, Miguel. You told me you would comfort me in my old age. Look at you, child. Look at you." The candles mocked her with their brightness and her child remained silent and naked on the dining room table.

Mama Chona wept for three days and three nights after he was in the ground and her children did not see her shed another tear for the rest of her life. "Life is suffering," she said to them. "Life is letting go of what you love."

With no end in sight to the Revolution after almost ten years, Jesus Angel decided to move his family to Juarez. He was surprised when his wife did not object.

"I will even cross the river into Texas," she told him. "I cannot bear this stupidity another day."

The Rio Grande—shallow, muddy, ugly in those places where the bridges spanned it—was a constant disappointment and hardly a symbol of the promised land to families like Mama Chona's. They had not sailed across an ocean or ridden in wagons and trains across half a continent in search of a new life. They were migrant, not immigrant, souls. They simply and naturally went from one bloody side of the river to the other and into a land that just a few decades earlier had been Mexico. They became border Mexicans with American citizenship.

Mama Chona felt the force of these historical conditions, even if she was not fully aware of them all or chose to ignore the more painful ones. Sensing that North America was a country devoted to the future, she was determined to instill in her children and theirs those values she cherished most. Caught between the future and the past, some of the Angels lived and died for the moment because they had to. The rest led double lives and followed the rules of both cultures as best they could.

In Mama Chona's eyes, theology was much more important than history. In the new life without her husband—his burial was the first ceremony she had to arrange in the strange and thorny place they had fled to—Mama Chona clung even more closely to the Catholic God she knew with absolute certainty ruled the universe.

Their flight northward, Jesus Angel's death, the way she saw her children treated by their Americanized neighbors and bosses were all part of God's plan for the Angels. She prayed she might live long enough to see the beatification, if not canonization, of one of her own.

In the meantime, Mama Chona saw that in a constant, not always bloodless struggle for power, the God who spoke English with a Texas accent was almost always victorious and rewarded His minions with better-paying jobs and more expensive homes in the nicer parts of town where the schools were better. The Catholic God of the migrants ordered His servants to multiply, and bided His time. Mama Chona vowed to wait by His side. "Thy will be done," she said to Him.

Eduviges waited along with her mother. She was the last of the children to marry. By the time she gave birth to her own daughters, it was clear to her that the Mexican and Anglo citizens of Del Sapo remained divided despite all the pretense and effort to make it an "All-American" city proud of its international connections.

As Eduviges and the century grew older and the real cowboys died out or rode on to wilder frontiers, Eduviges saw them replaced by those of the drugstore and bank variety. They took control of the town by making certain the water rights belonged only to a select few among them.

For the most part, Mexican Americans like her and her children were ignored or exploited. When they were educated into the lower middle class, their school lessons contained no mention of their heritage or contributions to history. Those in the working class remained desperate and poor despite their citizenship.

"God help my girls," Eduviges prayed.

vii

Encarnacion Olmeca—Mama Chona's maiden name—had been brought up and educated by Spanish nuns in Mexico before the turn of the century. She and her sister Refugio—Tia Cuca to the children—were taught the ways of Castilian ladies and to their dying day, they felt themselves to be aristocratic in spirit if not in actuality. Because she believed so deeply in her God, Mama Chona taught her children, especially the girls, to strike a rigid moral stance toward their adopted world. In this project, she felt her sister Cuca was no help at all.

"You are constantly undermining my authority over them," Encarnacion told her. They were sitting in Cuca's garden watching the hummingbirds zip in and out among the canna lilies.

"My goodness, Chona, you sound like a general." Cuca brushed away a fly with an exquisitely beautiful hand.

"I don't care what you think I sound like. You know I'm right. All you care about is their pleasure. I am more interested in their souls."

"Well, good for you, dear sister. More tea? It's real *yerba buena* from the garden."

Mama Chona was aided in her efforts to educate

her children's souls by a French Carmelite nun she had never met but whose reputation and life she used as the perfect model of the pure young woman who burns with love for Jesus.

She herself may have been Jesus Angel's wife and the mother of his ten children, but in her soul Jesus Christ was her master. Mama Chona did her duty on earth with her eyes toward heaven and she saw to it that her daughters and theirs followed her example. Even before she was made a saint, the Little Flower of Jesus became Mama Chona's most adored religious figure.

As if to vindicate Mama Chona's trust and devotion to her, Thérèse of Lisieux was canonized ten years after the Angel family's arrival on the border. Mama Chona made her the adopted patron saint of the family. For several years, the grandchildren were unable to tell the difference between the statue of Saint Thérèse and that of the Virgin Mary at the Cathedral and were constantly arguing about the roles of the two saintly women in the life of Jesus.

One day, Josie came up with a perfect solution to the problem of the statues. "Just remember," she said to her sisters and cousins, "that the Virgin Mary is not the one carrying those ugly lipstick-red roses."

To Mama Chona's daughters, however, the Carmelite saint was more than just a statue. She was what they were meant to be, and in the first years of their life in the desert, thinking about the Little Flower's physical suffering helped them put up with the stony conditions of their own childhood and adolescence. Later, such early training led Mama Chona's daughters to be greatly disappointed in men.

They had learned that the world was imperfect and that they must strive for perfection, spiritual if not actual, even if it killed them or deprived them of what they loved most in the world. Jesus Maria offered up her body to God on the day of her first communion. Eufemia Maria—in the desert, they began calling her Mema—offered her soul because she had already met and fallen in love with David Martinez and knew that her body would not be pure enough for God. Eduviges Maria kept her body and soul to herself and prayed that God and life would not force her to choose one at the expense of the other.

From their mothers—aided by a religion still stressing hell and damnation in Latin, English, and Spanish—the granddaughters learned that life in this human form was to be endured and that the only future that mattered was the after life. Mama Chona, their mothers told them, was a living example of such endurance and faith and, lest the girls be tempted by the pleasures of the world, they were reminded that suffering was a given and as timeless as the desert around them.

"God, what a world they've invented," Josie said to Serena. And once again, she made up her mind to leave it as soon as life gave her the chance.

"I can see why they did it," her sister said. "It kept them alive and going. Can you imagine what it must have been like for them before we were born? How in the world did they manage?"

"Well, maybe it worked for them," Josie said. "But I'll be damned if I'm going to live that way. And if I have any kids, I am not going to do to them what was done to us."

"Oh, Josie, has it been that awful?"

"Yes, it has been that awful. You're the saint, remember? Not me. Mother and Mama Chona have made that very clear."

The girls and their cousins watched Mama Chona live to be more than one hundred years old. They saw six of her ten children enter the afterlife ahead of her, most of them violently hurled to the other side of the grave before they were fifty. And in her senility, they heard Mama Chona call them by her own children's names.

"How dark the night is, Eduviges." Mama Chona spoke these words in Spanish to Josie, who already knew how dark the night could be, and was annoyed with the old lady for thinking she was in any way like her mother.

viii

After Serena "became a young woman" and Josie was about to cross that border, their mother was finishing yet one more description of the wicked world when their father surprised them by looking up from the weekly summary of his small gas station's receipts and saying to Eduviges as if the girls were out of the room, "They'll be okay if you stop bothering them with your hysterical notions about the world. I know you don't even believe in them and are just imitating your mother and sister for God knows what reason." Eduviges was struck dumb.

"All I ask," their father continued, stressing the I, "is that Ofelia find the right man to care for her and that Serena not grow up to be a nun or a drunk. But if she is to be one or the other, I hope she's a drunk because then there will be some hope for her."

The girls saw that the corners of his mouth were turned up and that he knew perfectly well they were in the room and all ears. He sucked in his cheeks, half lowered his eyelids, and gave them his armadillo look as a gift for having listened without interrupting him.

Sancho Salazar loved telling his wife and her sister Jesus Maria that all religions were the downfall of mankind and had caused the slaughter of untold millions in the name of gods whose disciples preached charity and practiced carnage. Ofelia and Serena ignored his tirades against the Church. Josie took them to heart and got into trouble by daring to argue with Sister Xavier during the weekly catechism lessons.

In their early adolescence, the girls learned that their father had been married and divorced before he met their mother. "I knew it," Josie said. "All those times Mother made me wait in the car while she went knocking on strangers' doors to find out where Daddy was. He must have been visiting *her.*"

Once, she had watched Eduviges let out the air in the tires of her father's car, parked in the northeast part of town in front of a lurid pink house almost covered by climbing red roses. Sancho had said nothing about it when he got home late for a supper his wife had left cold on the kitchen table.

"How's the Rose Lady, Daddy?" Josie had asked him with affection. He answered her with a melancholy silence.

Later that night, they overheard their mother's weepy recriminations and ultimatums. Their father remained silent and unrepentant.

"Do you think they had any children, Serena? Maybe we have a brother. Aren't you curious at all?" Josie could hardly contain herself.

"Poor Daddy," was all she had got out of Serena on the subject.

The rest of the Angels did not make much of Sancho's early indiscretion, for it was known that he had not married his first wife in the Church. Mostly, Mama Chona had worried that Eduviges was on her way to being an old maid, and she was pleased when Sancho Salazar strolled onto the scene, even if he was a divorced man and freethinker. She knew that her daughter would be able to keep him in line.

"As for Josie," Sancho went on, "she's got a will

made of iron. From your side of the family, no doubt, Vickie." The girls loved hearing him call their mother that. Something about the way he said it made them aware of yearnings within their own bodies. "I pity the poor guy who tries to tame her." Sancho winked at his rebellious daughter and blew her a kiss.

Josie and Serena were constantly amazed by how easily their father lived in a house full of women brought up on traditions he found ridiculous and stultifying. "It's because he loves Mother more than his own life," Serena said. Josie did not want to think about that.

Ofelia went off to spend the rest of the afternoon with Mama Chona. Serena hugged her father and went to help Eduviges in the kitchen. Josie stayed in the parlor with Sancho and pretended to read.

Unable to concentrate, she looked up from the book in her hands and out of the window. The cold, gray day offered them no rain and made the mountains a shade darker than the sky. The toad's eye was lost in the shadows. She went back to her reading.

The pages of the novel became wings that seemed to move of their own accord. Already, she was far enough along to identify with both the madwoman locked up in the attic and the governess she guessed would get "the" man in the end. She closed the book and looked outside once more. In the warmth of the room, Josie felt iron-gray February sliding toward the dust storms of March like her own will unable to control itself. For a long while after Sancho left her alone, she sat thinking about her father's view of her. She agreed with it.

ix

In high school, Josie began to see that she was not kind or charitable in the ways their mother taught them to be. Nor was she popular like her cousin Miguel Chico, two years younger than she and already a class favorite.

Even though he was one of Mama Chona's pets, Josie adored him. Together, they loved and argued about books and movies and from the start, felt they could talk honestly to each other about most family matters. Their intimacy was born when they discovered that each found the wicked stepmother far more interesting than the boring Snow White, who deserved her even more boring and bland prince.

"They're so nice, they make me sick," Josie told Miguel Chico.

"Me, too," he said. "Aren't we awful?"

Josie prided herself on her intelligence and on seeing the world without sentimentality or exaggeration. "I am the true scientist in this crazy family," she said to her cousin. "And the family, especially

Mother, won't forgive me because I tell them what I see, good and bad, without all that sugarcoating or denial."

Miguel Chico leaned to the clinical, if not the scientific, and took Josie's side in most family quarrels. Enjoying his popularity and the privileges of a favorite grandchild, he was still denying what he saw in himself, let alone others, in those early years of learning to be the consummate pleaser.

Josie watched him charm his life away through high school, where, with little effort, he carried off all the prizes. How she hated it when her mother pointed out his accomplishments to her. Only her sense that he was headed toward disaster kept alive her affection for him every time Eduviges asked, "Why can't you be like your cousin Miguel?"

"Hello, nephew," Eduviges said to him warmly. He and Josie were in the kitchen spreading apple butter on saltines. "How nice of you to stop by on your way home from school."

"Thank you, Tia. I hope we're not in your way," he said. Mama Chona had taught him the best of manners.

"Not at all, Miguelito. But Josie knows she's not supposed to eat between meals." She spoke as if her daughter were a stranger in the room. Miguel Chico put down the cracker he had just buttered.

"Not you, Miguel. You're a growing boy. You can eat as much as you want. It's only natural."

Josie had told him that morning that her mother

was launching a new antiweight campaign and starving them to death. Miguel Chico knew enough to keep quiet when Josie fought with Eduviges in his presence. Out of the corner of his eye, he saw his cousin pop another buttered saltine into her mouth.

"Ofelia and Serena understand why I ask them to be careful about what and when they eat," his aunt said, looking at him with dark, clear eyes from behind cheekbones that were sharply elegant. "Do you think I'm being unreasonable?"

Her nephew mumbled something noncommittal and was glad when his aunt and cousin did not ask him to repeat it. He felt the kitchen charged with their antagonism toward each other, very like when he was in his father's presence. Here, he was an observer, but he lost his appetite in an instant. Josie fixed three more crackers and offered him one. He took it and set it next to the other on the blue napkin in his lap.

"Eat, cousin," she said. "You have permission from on high." And she put the two remaining snacks in her mouth at the same time.

"Josie, I'm warning you," Eduviges said. "If you don't feel like eating your supper later, there won't be any midnight raids on the refrigerator."

"What are you going to do, Mother? Put a padlock on the door?" Josie laughed.

"*Malcriada,*" her mother said. "Ofelia and Serena know I mean it."

Josie licked the apple butter on the spoon. "It sure

is hard," she said to Miguel Chico, "being the sister of a perfect child and a saint." Then, looking at her mother with even darker eyes, she said, "Leave me alone, Mother. I'm old enough to make my own choices. And anyway, you're never going to approve of anything I do, so why not just give up and be quiet about it? I'll feel your disapproval. How's that? Just don't make me listen to it."

Miguel Chico sat stunned by the boldness of his cousin's words. He knew it was a habit of the older generation of Angels to tell everyone else but one's own children how much they loved them and how proud they were of their accomplishments. Always, they made their own feel that nothing they did would ever be good enough. Miguel Chico's father was a master at that game. Still, he had never spoken to him in such a tone and with such harsh words.

"Well," Eduviges said. "Just remember that I warned you, young lady. Please come back and see us, Miguel. You are always welcome in my house." She left the room.

"I think you're going to hear from Saint Wretched," Miguel Chico said to his cousin after putting back the top on the apple-butter jar.

"Oh, shut up," Josie said. "Why didn't you eat the crackers, Mr. Perfect?"

"Because I wasn't hungry," he said.

"Neither was I after she started giving orders. I don't know why I kept on feeding my face like that. I feel sick."

"Saint Wretched knows. I leave you to your misery, cousin. Call me later when you're hungry and I'll describe all your favorite foods to you."

"Go away and leave me alone."

"Yes, your majesty."

"And don't call me that." She was on the verge of tears.

Miguel Chico, sensing that nothing was going to work, went home.

The following night, they sat in the half-light that flickered from the screen above them. The most beautiful woman in the world was dying in the arms of her lover and Josie was struck by a fit of weeping. Tearless, Miguel Chico wondered how such a sappy story could make him feel so thirsty.

Behind them, other students from the high school were yawning or necking or telling others to be quiet. Josie, usually curious about who was doing what with whom, did not notice. All she heard was the coughing that caused the woman on the screen to cringe and bend in awful ways and still look gorgeous. In his panic, her lover, also gorgeous, yelled for the nurse. At last, he had realized the woman loved him and only him.

Until the final scene, Josie and Miguel Chico sat transfixed by the black-and-white figures floating above them like spirits in the dark. Their interest in old movies made them feel special, but they did not imagine they would be so captivated by this one. Before that night, they had never seen such a man or woman on the screen.

The woman was so purely beautiful that only

nakedness would have done justice to her. No one but the Legion of Decency would have thought her immodest, not even Josie's mother. Instead, they saw the actress bogged down by dresses that hung limply from her thin, translucent shoulders, and until the end, Miguel Chico smiled at the hairdos, which made the woman look slightly ridiculous. Only her voice and the way she moved kept him from laughing out loud. She was like an animal trapped in a cage.

Lencho Gonzalez and other members of the Fatherless Gang were making obscene noises and eating popcorn and chewing gum so that they could be heard all the way to the balcony. The Valley Theater was on their turf, and they went to every movie to make sure all outsiders understood they owned the territory. "Hey, man, she's too skinny," Lencho said for all to hear.

The skinny woman, head bent back, neck arching toward her lover's face, was taking a last breath. The theater was completely quiet. All of them had known from the moment they saw her that she was going to die. Nothing that beautiful could possibly live. She belonged to another world. Beside her in the half-light, Josie heard her cousin snickering. She pinched him hard.

"What's the matter with you?" she asked him as they walked up the aisle toward the side exit.

Just ahead of them, Lencho turned to his girl-friend and said, "Maybe if she'd ate something, she wouldn't of died." He laughed. The girlfriend punched him.

"How could you laugh? I wanted to kill you," Josie said to her cousin. "I haven't had such a good cry in ages."

"I know. You scared me and that's why I started to laugh. I thought you were going to pass out. I was looking at you and hearing her. What a voice she has!"

"Well, I'll never forgive you. Did I hurt your arm?"

"Yes. I'll probably die."

"Oh, shut up."

The truth was that he had been watching Josie because he had become infected by the woman's suffering. All tragedy affected him in that way. He could tolerate such pain for only so long before he had to breathe normally and remind himself to laugh or smile.

He and Josie had founded the Order of Saint Wretched so that they might laugh at misery. Passion, betrayal, unrequited love were all offered up to Saint Wretched whenever the cousins found themselves or others once again enthralled by the sins of the flesh. Their favorite characters and writers were on the list of the suffering, and they spoke of them as living members of the Order. He knew Josie was going to want to include the skinny actress.

Once a month, they sent anonymous cards to friends and relatives in anguish or, on boring months, to those who were living lives that seemed remote and fated to the cousins. The cards informed them of their honorary status in the Order.

When they sent one to their aunt Jesus Maria, she mistook it for a chain letter and threw it away. For the rest of that week, she ran into bad luck everywhere she turned, even at the local Safeway. Counting out her pennies—she loved being exact even if she made others wait in line—she dropped her coin purse, saw her daily savings roll and scatter, and was certain that the man behind her had taken two quarters.

"I saw him put them in his pocket, children. And when he smiled at me like the Devil, I knew he had done it. I should have done what that letter said," Jesus Maria added as if to herself.

"What did it say?" Josie asked her. She was sitting on the hassock by Jesus Maria's pale green chair. Miguel Chico was at the piano across the room. He stopped playing when he heard his aunt mention the letter. They were visiting their cousin Rudy, Jesus Maria's second to last child, who was in bed with a bad head cold. The three cousins had made their first communion together. Without telling them why, Rudy had refused to become a member of the Order. Josie and Miguel Chico made him swear not to mention Saint Wretched's existence to anyone. They threatened him with the wire hanger tickle torture.

"What did the letter say, Tia?" Josie asked again

in a slower, louder way. She knew her aunt was partly deaf.

Jesus Maria faced her and said in Spanish, "Oh, I don't remember. Something about suffering out loud. To tell you the truth, I didn't read it all the way through. Father McGovern devoted part of his sermon last Sunday to chain letters. They are a sin and objects of the Devil." She sat straight up in her chair and challenged Satan to enter her house.

"Don't stop playing, Miguelito. I wish Rudy had kept up with his lessons. I've despaired that any of my children will ever amount to anything." She spoke this untruth loudly and toward the room where Rudy lay asleep. Her oldest son, Gaspar, was the first Ph.D. in the family, but because he had left Del Sapo and lived in Chicago, Jesus Maria ignored his existence.

Miguel Chico went on playing a simple melody filled with Polish melancholy. He stopped when he heard Josie say, "Oh, Tia, they're just stupid letters written by people who are bored with their own lives. Isn't that so, Mickie?" He sat on his hands and said nothing.

"No, Josie, Father McGovern is right. They are messages from Hell and I was right to throw it away." All the Angel children knew that Jesus Maria divided the world into right and wrong, good and evil, light and darkness. She seemed to know nothing about the grayness in which most of them wandered about feeling ashamed of themselves for not seeing life as clearly as she or Mama Chona.

"Please, Miguelito, play more of that melody."
The children also knew how much she loved music.

"What do you think of chain letters, cousin?"
Josie asked him. She sensed he was making deals
with his guilt and wanted him to laugh at it with her.

Sitting on the bench in the perpetual twilight of
their aunt's parlor, Miguel Chico felt trapped. If he
joined his cousin in the fun, the crow at the back of
his neck would dig more deeply into his brain. If he
told his aunt the truth, both she and Josie would be
angry with him and the hummingbirds would eat
away at his heart.

"Not much," he said, and went back to the melody. It helped keep the birds away.

"Chicken," Josie said.

"What did you say, Josefa?" Jesus Maria asked.

"Nothing, Tia. Just talking to myself as usual."
Miguel Chico pretended he had not heard her.
Already, in his early teens, he was addicted to guilt.

Rudy called to them. "Keep playing, Miguel,"
Jesus Maria told him. "Josie, help me make your sick
cousin a hot lemonade."

"My father puts a little bourbon in it for us,"
Josie said. "He says it kills the germs."

"Your father is going to turn you girls into
drunks. Just plain honey will be enough for Rudy."
She asked her niece to slice the lemons.

X

Josie met Harold Newman at a high school dance that was almost called off because of a late September thunderstorm. She asked Miguel Chico to be her escort. He was now tall enough to dance with her and old enough to drive his father's '51 Chevy. They both loved to mambo and jitterbug. Rock-and-roll and the cha-cha were less than a year away.

"You look like a birthday cake," her cousin said when Josie walked into her mother's living room wearing six starched crinolines under a light blue dress that flared out from the waist and down around her legs. The dance was semiformal, and Josie had on her comfortable loafers and soft white cotton socks rolled three times at the ankle.

"I want to dance and dance. Let's go before Mother changes her mind and makes me stay home," she said in whisper.

"You'd better get a sweater. It's really blowing out there and smelling like rain." In a new navy blue suit, Miguel Chico looked even more slender to her. Josie thought him the most handsome of her cousins, even if he did have to wear glasses to recognize her from across the room.

"I'll be right back. Mother's in the kitchen. Go

61

talk her out of believing we're going to get killed in your dad's car. She actually wanted to drive us herself. Can you believe it?"

His aunt was making *mole poblano* and the smell of red *chile* was beginning to fill the house. Squares of the Mexican chocolate she used in the sauce were melting slowly into an ancient small pot on the stove. Its fragrance joined the red pepper smell in Miguel Chico's nose and made his mouth water.

"Hello, Miguel. I'd hug you but my hands are full of *chile.* Sit down. Would you like something to drink?"

"No, thank you, Tia. There's going to be a lot to eat and drink at the dance. And you don't have to worry. I'll watch out for Josie. She'll be all right." She was handwringing the toasted red peppers into a strainer and using an old wooden spoon to force the mush into a large pan.

"This is the best *chile* from Juarez we've had in a long time. The *mole* will be ready when you and Josie get back. It only takes a few hours."

"We might be a little longer than that. I'm on the social committee this year and I'll have to help clean up."

"Are you sure you don't want me to take you? Josie's father can come for the two of you whenever you say."

"We'll be fine, Tia. I've got my license and I've been driving for three months by myself. Please don't worry."

Josie came in with a beaded white sweater around her shoulders. "Let's go, cousin," she said. "I want to watch everyone come in. Good-bye, Mother. We'll be back soon."

Eduviges had rinsed her hands and was wiping them dry. They were still red and would remain *chile-* stained for a few days. She claimed the warmth was good for her arthritis. "Let me take you."

"Mother, please don't start. We've already been over this. Come on, Miguel, before she chains us to the sink."

"Really, Tia, I'll be careful and we'll be back by eleven. I promise."

Eduviges was following them to the front door as if ready to go with them. Miguel Chico bumped into her when he turned suddenly and walked over to the dining room table. He picked up a small white box that he handed to Josie with an exaggerated bow. "Here, your majesty. I almost forgot to give you these." It was a corsage of pink carnations.

"Thank you, cousin. They're beautiful. Look, Mother." Eduviges barely glanced at the flowers and was looking hard at Josie's face. She was wearing lipstick. Usually, Josie waited until she was out of the house before putting it on. Quickly, she turned away and saw herself reflected in the mirror by the door. "I never know where to put these things. No matter where I pin them, they get in the way. I know, I'll put them in my hair." In the mirror, Josie saw her mother's face, eyes bulging and jaws shut tightly, perched on her left shoulder. "Here, cousin, help me," she said and handed him some bobby pins from her purse.

"I'll help you," Eduviges said, her owl's face dropping out of the mirror.

"No, Mother, let Miguel do it. He's taller. Your hands smell like *chile* and I don't want my hair to reek of it. I just know my clothes smell like it already."

As Miguel adjusted the flowers in his cousin's hair, the lights dimmed. A lightning storm was passing over them. A clap of thunder made the house vibrate.

"Oh, sweet Jesus, Mary, and Joseph," Eduviges said. Josie ignored her.

"There," Miguel Chico said. "All done. Hold them until we get to the car or they'll be ruined." She barely heard him through the noise of the thunder, which she was pretending not to notice.

"I don't think you should go out at all in this storm," Eduviges said.

"We're going," Josie said, one hand on her head, the other pushing Miguel Chico out of the house. A crooked spear of lightning hit a telephone pole down the street and turned the night into bleached white day.

"God be with you," Eduviges said, sending them off into eternity.

"Come on," Josie shouted, taking Miguel Chico's hand and leading him down the walk toward the car. The wind blew her dress in all directions.

"Keep your skirt down," she heard her mother shout. The thunder was beating open the sky, but Josie felt only a few drops of rain on her face before getting into the car.

Adjusting her hair in the rearview mirror, she said, "I thought we'd never get out of there. Quick, before she decides to follow us."

A few moments later, the downpour began in sheets of rain driven by wind that made it difficult for Miguel Chico to see more than five feet away. Instantly, the gutters became rushing streams that flowed halfway into the streets at each corner. Thunder and lightning were one and the cousins were not able to hear the radio. Some drivers had pulled over to the side of the road.

"Maybe we should stop until the storm passes," Miguel said. He was awed by the force of the wind and rain.

"No, no," Josie said, intoxicated by the smell of the wet sagebrush and Vitex trees that lined the street. "I don't want to get there late. Just watch out for the idiots who can't drive in this town when it rains." She almost offered to take the wheel, but thought that she might be acting too much like her mother if she said anything. "Go on. You're doing just fine. This will stop in a minute."

Despite the flashflooding of some streets along the way, they arrived at the gymnasium on time. Miguel Chico immediately went to check on the food. It had arrived intact, but he found out from

Jimmy Sherman, the president of the student council, that the small band they had hired was stranded on the Las Cruces highway. They had already rigged up the school record player to the P.A. system, and each member of the social committee was to take turns playing the seventy-eights and forty-fives available in the record library.

"What a bore," Miguel Chico said. "We'll put everyone to sleep."

"Don't worry. I've already called Mimi and Harriet Reigel. They've got all the latest records. I'll make a speech about it."

"Not too long, Jimmy. Remember this is a dance. You've already been elected." Two years later, Miguel Chico was to be the second Mexican American in the history of the school elected to serve as president of the council. "Make sure they bring "Earth Angel" and "Cherry Pink and Apple Blossom White" and whatever that new guy Elvis has done. I'll take the first shift playing the music." He went to find Josie and was glad to see that the storm had not kept too many people away.

She was waiting for him not far from the entrance where she could get a good look at what the other girls were wearing. Most of them—Mexican and Anglo—wore the crinolines just starting to become popular, their hair short, socks rolled tightly around the ankles. In identical angora sweaters and tight skirts, Bobba Hatfield and her best friend, Mary Anne Shapiro, walked in with their escorts.

"Poor Mary Anne," Miguel Chico said to Josie. "What's she going to do when Bobba graduates this year?"

"Walk around in sackcloth and ashes probably. God, Bobba is gorgeous. She's got the figure for that skirt. Did you see Blanca? She's here with Manny. I didn't know they were going out." She looked down at her own skirt and thought that for once she was dressed in style. Her mother taught them that clothes were a necessity, not a pleasure. All those crinolines filled her with guilty delight.

"They're not," Miguel Chico said in a voice full of innuendo. "I'll tell you all about it later. Right now, we've got to get this party going. What do you want to hear first?"

"Anything. Just hurry and do what you have to do so that we can dance."

She watched him make his way through the clusters of students waiting to hear what Jimmy Sherman was going to tell them. As usual, she saw that the Mexicans and Anglos formed separate groups. Her cousin bounced with ease from one group to another and was friendly to everyone, sometimes insincerely, Josie knew. His smile and wit opened doors that warned others to stay out. Though she envied his popularity and social grace, Josie thought her cousin one of the loneliest people in the world.

Crossovers from one group to another were noticed and talked about later, for each race guarded its own and had been taught to fear the consequences of mixing cultures. An undeclared borderline existed between Mexicans and Anglos that only a few dared to cross in the name of love. The occasional mixed couple, usually an Anglo girl with a Mexican boy, kept its distance and was content to be young and uncaring about what life in a border town had in store for the two of them.

Just the year before, there was a scandal when one of the Anglo girls had to marry a Mexican boy. Her father had gone into the principal's office unannounced and shouted out his accusations so that all could hear how his daughter was ruined for all time. Both young people had to leave school and the town.

"They're better off getting out of here. Imagine that poor baby's life in this town full of hypocrites," Josie said. Her honesty made her unpopular and she knew it. When Miguel Chico was told about the doomed couple, he looked very concerned and then smiled without saying a word. Later that year, he was elected class favorite.

A scratchy Glenn Miller record came through the loudspeakers and was occasionally overwhelmed by the thunder rolling overhead. Several couples began to jitterbug on the highly polished floor. The girls' crinolines were reflected on its surface as they twirled back and forth like tops with arms. Those without partners gathered along the walls—the girls talking in giggly ways to each other, the boys silent and observant, screwing up their courage.

Waiting to be asked to dance was Josie's idea of

hell, and she walked to the buffet table hoping to run into someone she knew well enough to ask him herself. She bumped into Doris Hansen.

"Sorry, Doris," Josie said into a pair of albino eyes. "I didn't see you."

"It was my fault," Doris said in a voice that insisted and apologized at the same time. Josie was trapped.

Doris was the plainest girl in the school and students spread rumors about her uncleanliness. Josie looked at the faded pink dress, unpressed and hanging loosely from Doris' high waist. Its short sleeves were worn through and revealed the boniest shoulders Josie had ever seen. Doris crossed her arms in front of her and placed a hand on each shoulder. Embarrassed, Josie looked down. Doris' old and cracked black patent-leather shoes were soaked and her ankles spattered with mud.

"I stepped in a puddle," Doris said. "The flowers in your hair look nice."

"Thanks. My cousin gave them to me."

Doris' reddish-blond hair was fixed permanently into two thin braids pinned tightly to the top of her head, which made Josie think of misplaced and mistreated children. When they were in the seventh grade, Lencho Gonzalez thought he saw the freckles on Doris' forehead move, pointed toward them, and yelled out, "Cooties!" The name stuck and that was what they called her, not always behind her back.

Nat "King" Cole began singing to them and Josie

looked for someone to rescue her. She did not want to spend any part of the evening feeling sorry for anyone.

"My father made me come," Doris said quietly. "He says I spend too much time by myself." The rims of her eyelids were a bright red. "He got Roger Kemendo to bring me. Can I stay with you until he comes back from the restroom?"

"Of course, Doris. Let's go eat something." Josie led the way.

The storm was blowing away from them and only an occasional lightning flash dimmed the lights and turned the dancers into black and gray shadows. Just as she and Doris reached the table, a thunderclap shook the building and the lights went out completely. Josie heard the music groan into silence and the giggles and shuffling of the students around her. The chaperones began shouting for everyone to stay where they were and not panic.

Another sheet of lightning lit up the room and was followed quickly by a long roll of thunder that signaled the end of the storm. The air in the room was heavy with the smell of greasewood and sage. Looking for Doris, Josie turned and saw the shadow of a young man standing a few feet away from her. He was in an R.O.T.C. uniform.

"How melodramatic," Josie said.

The lights came back on and the music started up where it had left off. Doris was nowhere to be seen.

"What did you say?" the young man asked her.

His eyes were on the dancers and looked at her only when he spoke. His thin, angular face and small features pleased her.

"I was wondering why lightning and thunder are so corny," she said and saw Miguel Chico making his way toward them.

"Would you like to dance?" the young man asked. "My name is Harold Newman. I think we're in the same track of classes this year. I noticed you and your cousin at the movies a lot this summer. You must like them."

"Yes, very much. Let's dance." Josie knew who he was and had caught him staring at her from a distance several times. She had looked up his picture in the yearbook and had hoped they were in the same class. She tried not to think that her mother would approve of his high forehead and light skin.

Before Miguel Chico reached them, they were in the middle of the dance floor. Kitty Kallen was singing about how much the little things meant as Harold led Josie in a slow dance. He was not as good a dancer as her cousin, but he guided her well enough so that she sensed where to place her own feet. Once, she miscalculated and stepped on his boot.

"Sorry," she said.

"For what?"

"I stepped on you," she said and caught herself thinking something quite different altogether. She was vaguely aware that she was flirting with him. Just that morning, Josie had told Serena to slap her if she ever saw her doing that. "I can't stand how silly teenage girls talk. They sound like Aunt Trini's parakeets in heat." Aunt Trini was an Angel by marriage. To Harold she said, "Didn't you feel me step on you?"

"No. I was smelling the flowers in your hair. They're nice," he added simply.

Later, after a jitterbug, two more ballads, and the bunny hop, Josie excused herself. "I've got to find my cousin," she said.

"All right," Harold said and disappointed her with his casual tone. She was smiling more at herself than at him and thought she was a dumb teenager after all.

"See you in class," she said, shook his hand, and left him standing in the middle of the dance floor.

Miguel Chico was taking his turn serving punch at the far end of the gym. Almost all the food was gone and the crepe paper decorations were stained with *chili con queso* and barbecue sauce. Because of his big ears, the grin on his face seemed wider than usual to Josie.

"Well, do you know him?" she asked.

"Not really. I don't go for military types."

"I'm serious, cousin. Tell me what you know." She looked at the couples still dancing and saw that Harold was jitterbugging with Marguerite Moya.

"Want me to go beat her up?" Miguel Chico asked.

"Why on earth would you do that?"

" 'Jealousy! night and day you torture me!' " he sang.

Josie smiled. Miguel Chico used to win the talent contests at all their childhood birthday parties singing that stupid song. "You're crazy," she said. "He seems like a nice guy, that's all."

"I guess so. You've spent the whole night dancing with him and I'm going to tell your mother. She'll be happy to know the love of your life has an Anglo name."

"His mother is Mexican. He saw me talking to Doris and told me only his mother would be that kind. What do you think about that?"

"Is he Catholic?" Miguel Chico asked, imitating their aunt Jesus Maria's tone.

"Of course," Josie said. She was lying. She had not even thought to ask Harold that question.

"Same soap opera, different characters," Miguel Chico said. "Dance the last dances with me, cousin. Let's go show them how."

"Okay, but don't get too close to him. I don't want him to think I'm chasing him."

"Calm down. I know what I'm doing. I've read *Modern Romance.*"

Miguel Chico led her past Harold and his partner to a spot on the dance floor where she could see him out of the corner of her eye. Even at that distance, Harold's presence was palpable to her, and once again a strange thought she had while dancing with him floated into her mind like a mist. She missed a beat and came out of a turn facing away from her cousin. She felt everyone was watching her.

"Over here," Miguel Chico said and deftly led her back into the dance. "Dream dancing?"

The mist inside her head became a fog and she abandoned herself to the dance. A few moments later, in the middle of another romantic ballad, she and Harold brushed elbows behind their partners' backs. Josie bent her head back and laughed.

"You look goofy," Miguel Chico said. "What's the matter with you?"

"Nothing," she said. She saw two children coming toward her out of the fog. They jumped up and down and waved. "Oh, my God," she said aloud.

"What? Something wrong?" her cousin asked.

"No. Just thinking something stupid. I'll tell you later." The fog and children dissolved and she did not see Harold anywhere near them. Josie was relieved and made it through the last dance quite naturally.

But when the lights brightened and couples began leaving the floor in greater numbers, Josie felt a great longing to see Harold one more time. As if summoned, he stood before her and was saying good night in a quiet almost inaudible way to her.

Miguel Chico waited until Harold walked away before he spoke. "Well, well, well. Now, I am not only going to tell your mother, I'm telling your father. You know I'm supposed to protect you from horrible men who only want one thing."

"He's not like that," Josie said.

"God, you are hooked. I was only kidding."

"Take me home," she said. "I'm tired. What time is it, anyway?"

"You don't want to know," Miguel Chico said and then told her it was after midnight. "Your mother is going to kill me."

"Don't worry. I'll go in by myself. I don't care what she says or does." She began to roll down the window and stopped when Harold's face appeared in the night on the other side of the glass. "Stay there," she said.

"What?" her cousin asked.

"Nothing," she said.

Josie's eyelids grew heavier and she fought against sleep by silently counting every other streetlight on the way to her mother's house. Only the reflection of the traffic signals in a few puddles reminded her of the storm and she felt herself floating in a calm unknown to her, safe and unreachable. From a great distance, she heard Miguel Chico humming the summer's most popular tune.

"I can't get that song out of my mind," he said and began to sing the words of the chorus.

The melody brought her back to the dry and vast bottom of a prehistoric sea. Josie opened the window and stuck her head into the cool desert air. She let it undo her hair and the flowers fell away into the night.

"God, I love this smell," she said.

xi

Five years later, she married Harold in the Cathedral on the hottest day of the year. Josie's uncles Miguel Grande and his older brother, Felix, drove the wedding party to the church in identical four-door, pink and white '55 Chevys.

Dressed in mint green satin and holding a bouquet of miniature bright red roses, Serena was her maid of honor. Miguel Chico was an usher and happy not to have to wear one of the lilac-colored tuxedos Josie chose for the groomsmen in a rebellious move to put some color into the traditional rite. The bridesmaids were in pale peach-colored dresses and carried sprays of small flowers dyed to match the men's outfits.

"I want us to look like Easter eggs," Josie had said two and a half months earlier at the first fitting of her wedding dress.

"What you are going to look is ridiculous," her mother said in Spanish.

"Do brides always have to wear white?"

"You know they do and you know why, Josefa."

"No, I don't, Mama. Tell us."

Eduviges' face reddened and she looked at the dress patterns spread out on the kitchen table. "They must have long sleeves. You know that women are supposed to cover their arms and heads whenever they are in church."

"This is my wedding, Mother, and I am not about to wear long sleeves in the middle of the summer. It's bad enough that I have to wear stockings nobody's going to see underneath all that material." Josie wanted a simple, form-fitting dress. Eduviges was insisting on a more traditional and elaborate design.

"The whole family will be there and I want you to be married in the proper way, Josie."

"What you mean is that you want to make sure they think I'm still a virgin. Should I wear a sign?"

They compromised. The bridesmaids' dresses had sleeves to the elbow. Josie's gown had short sleeves and was complicated everywhere else. "There. Are you happy?" she asked her mother. "I don't know how I'm supposed to move in this thing. If the sleeves weren't short, I'd feel completely embalmed."

Her mother was helping Monica the seamstress pin the hem. "When you see the photographs," she said through a mouthful of pins, "you'll thank me. Except for the sleeves, it's a beautiful dress. Monica has magical hands."

"Mama, don't talk with those things in your mouth," Serena said.

"Of course you do, Monica," Josie said, looking down at them. "I just wanted a simpler dress, that's all. But in this family, it's never mattered what I want."

"Well," Serena said, helping Josie adjust the veil,

which turned out to be too long in the front. "Soon you'll have a family of your own and can do what you want. Mother, will you please take those pins out of your mouth? I want to go to a wedding, not a funeral."

"Really, Mother?" Josie said, looking into her sister's eyes. "Is it true what Serena says? Will I be able to bring up my children the way I want and not according to the Middle Ages?"

"Your husband will have something to say about that," Eduviges said and backed away from her to inspect the hem. "Josie, are you standing on one foot? You look crooked."

"Oh, Mama, I'll always look that way to you. Serena, tell her it's the hem and not me."

"I am not speaking to her until she gets those pins out of her mouth. I don't want to kill her. Mother, please."

The women teased each other late into that April afternoon. Josie's wedding was still far enough away to seem like any other day to them.

Their aunt Sally surprised them all by arriving from Los Angeles a week before the ceremony. Not trusting her mother to do it, Josie had mailed the invitation to California without expecting a response. She was overjoyed when Sally phoned her from Miguel Grande's house to tell her she had returned to Del Sapo to make certain that her niece knew what she was doing. In those days, marrying in the Church meant marrying for all eternity.

"Oh, Aunt Sally, you're the best wedding present

of all. And I am sure. Wait till you meet him. He's an angel, not an Angel."

A member of the family by marriage, Aunt Sally was half Irish and half Mexican. She spoke Spanish and English with ease and delighted her nieces and nephews by holding her own in family discussions. Sitting in their parlors, tiny feet dangling a few inches above their carpets, freckles dancing along the backs of her arms and hands and all over her face, Sally reduced even Jesus Maria to silence by doggedly insisting on facts.

"No, Jessie," she said at the rehearsal dinner, "you're not that young. Did you give birth to Gaspar when you were twelve years old? I was at your wedding, remember?" She laughed in the joyless, angry way of those who have been disappointed in love. Only her Irish eyes, a gift from her father, sparkled with affection for them all.

When her husband, Armando, the black sheep in Mama Chona's family, took Sally and their two sons away from the desert in 1938, the rest of the family was relieved. "They belong in California," Mama Chona said and was glad she did not have to watch her honey-haired, green-eyed son destroy himself in a lifelong search for ecstasy.

For fifteen years, Sally watched him and did what she could to keep him away from the bottles of lost dreams he hid all over their apartment on Second Street in East Los Angeles. "Why do you drink so much, Armando?" she asked him only once.

"I'm looking for something," he said, staring out

79

at the birds-of-paradise blooming wildly against their next door neighbor's wall.

"What are you looking for? Tell me. I'll help you."

"It's there in those flowers. They won't let me in. I was there and now they won't let me in."

Sally had felt the day grow close around them. His matter-of-fact tone frightened her and she was aware of the smell of smog in her kitchen.

"Paradise, *querida,*" he said and poured himself another glass of gin. "Paradise."

"Don't worry, Mando. You're going to get there quicker than you can imagine. Please stop before the kids get home from school. All right?"

"I'll do better than that," he said calmly. "I'll leave."

"Fine. Do what you want."

That time he had left for three weeks and returned at dawn surrounded by mariachis singing and playing her favorite ballad. In a tearful rush of pity and affection, she let him come back to her once more. He was wearing his long white apron and smelled of freshly baked bread. He promised never to drink again.

Josie only remembered that her uncle Armando smelled like sour apples and was impressed by how quickly she learned to name the capitals of every state in the Union. Each visit, he made her begin with Nebraska. When he died of liver complications in his early forties, Josie was the youngest of the Angels in the caravan that made its way from the desert to his funeral in the City of the Angels. Mama Chona was the oldest and it was her last long journey on earth.

Now, Sally was sitting at Josie's end of the long table Juanita had set in her patio for the bridal shower. Instead of *mariachis,* she had hired an accordionist from Juarez to play quietly so that the guests could talk without shouting. Josie sat between Serena and Aunt Sally. Juanita knew how much the Angels feared Sally's tongue, especially in any arguments about the origins of the family.

It was reported to them that during the Zoot Suit riots in Los Angeles, Aunt Sally had ordered her sons not to deny their Mexican heritage at school. If they got beaten up for it, she told them, it would be less painful than what she would do to them when they got home.

"How are your boys?" Aunt Trini was asking Sally from across the table. She already knew that one of them was "in trouble" and that the other was studying to be a doctor.

"They're fine, Trinidad. And yours? Josie, pass me the *salsa,* will you?"

Josie and Serena exchanged glances. Almost every word their aunt Trini uttered was a monument to stupidity or illusion, and they sensed that Aunt Sally was ready to slug her each time she opened her mouth. Instead, because she had promised Juanita earlier that day to be good and keep her own mouth shut, she asked Josie about Harold. "He seems nice,

Josie," Sally said, ignoring Trinidad's report on her children's progress. "He's very quiet."

"That's what everybody says. But don't worry. He talks plenty when we're alone. You'll love his imitations of some of the people in this crazy family."

"Which ones?" Aunt Trini asked, interrupting herself and sliding into baby talk. "Come on, Josie, tell your aunt Trini."

"I'm so glad you came, Aunt Sally," Josie said. Serena was pinching her leg under the table.

"Yes. Me, too. Though I see this town hasn't changed in all the years I've been away. I hope you and Harold aren't staying here."

"Of course they are," Trinidad said. "This is a wonderful town." Half a taco disappeared into her face.

"I wonder how wonderful it would be if the guys who control the water department stopped putting lithium in it," Sally said with mock innocence.

"Are you saying they put drugs in our water?" Trini asked, truly horrified.

"Yes. So that you'll all stay nice and happy and obedient." She laughed.

Juanita heard her sister-in-law's laughter and instantly left the kitchen to join them. "Anybody need anything?" she asked, standing behind Sally's chair.

"No, *comadre,* I was just talking about how good the water is here. It tastes like something." And she laughed again.

"We want to move to California, Aunt Sally, but who knows where the army will send Harold. I've almost got my counseling credential and that will get me a job anywhere we go, I hope."

"Isn't that wonderful," Trini said. "In my day, all a woman could do was stay home and be a good wife and mother. You young people are so well educated now." The young women knew where she stood in the conflict between family and career that was beginning in their generation.

"Having an Anglo name will help you get a better job," Trini added.

The accordion was serenading them with the Mexican ballad Armando used to have the *mariachis* play for Sally. She rose from the table. "Excuse me," she said and walked into the house.

"What's wrong with her?" Aunt Trini asked Josie.

"Nothing, Tia," Serena said before her sister could answer. "Why don't you have another taco?"

"I shouldn't, but they are very good, Juanita. I like to put more cumin in the meat, myself. It brings out the flavor." She helped herself to the last two tacos on the platter.

Josie stood. "I hate cumin," she said. She kissed Juanita on the cheek. "Thanks. They were perfect and if I eat another bite, I won't fit into that dress Mother is making me put on next Saturday. I'll go find Sally."

On that morning in late June, Josie's side of the

Cathedral was filled with Angels. Harold's relatives and friends were scattered in clusters all over their side of the main aisle so that the empty spaces in the pews seemed all the larger to Miguel Chico. Ushering them in, he saw them more as passersby than as family witnesses to the eternal union of a man and a woman in holy matrimony.

Harold's mother kept shifting her hand from one place to another along Miguel Chico's arm as he escorted her to her place in the front pew across the aisle from his aunt Eduviges. Both women wore champagne colored dresses with hats that looked as if they had fallen accidentally onto their heads from the branches of trees unknown on earth.

In the choir loft, old Modesta Gonzalez was playing traditional wedding music on the new church organ with a gusto calculated to impress Father Vandermeer who, she was certain, was urging Monsignor to replace her with a younger and more energetic musician. Already, Modesta had missed several sharps and flats. Miguel Chico winced and put his hands over his ears.

"God, you'd think she could play them in her sleep by now," he said to the bridesmaids. "She's driving everyone crazy. It sounds like the start of a holy war." Some of the young women giggled. He walked toward Josie.

"Most people are seated now, cousin. I'll give the signal to the phantom upstairs whenever you're ready." He was trying very hard to appear nonchalant. That morning he had awakened with a knot of sadness in his belly and had not been able to eat the eggs Juanita scrambled for him.

"I'm ready," Josie said. "See if you can get the phantom to tone it down."

Everyone knew that Modesta was very proud of her thirty years' devotion to the Cathedral and for attending more masses than the priests themselves. In a moment of weakness, Monsignor Caffrey had given her an extra key to the lower steeple door so that she could practice whenever she wished. From the start of her long service, she often surprised the altar boys with her loud attempts to master unfamiliar works. They began calling her the phantom of the opera.

"God, I didn't even know she was there," Rudy had told his cousin Miguel Chico after a Friday afternoon novena. "I almost wet my pants and set fire to the altar when I was lighting the candles. I've never heard such a noise."

Waiting in the heat of the vestibule, Josie prepared herself for Modesta's assault on her nerves. She saw Serena and the bridesmaids at the side entrances making adjustments to their hair and dresses. Already, they looked like wilting bouquets.

When her cousin Yerma, Felix's oldest daughter, began a solitary, shaky walk down the center aisle toward the altar, Josie felt the beating of her heart for the first time that day. She always pitied the bridesmaids at any wedding. They seemed so unnecessary, like extra fingers or toes.

Josie and her father took the last of the Kleenex

from the box Serena had thought to bring and patted each other's faces with the damp tissues. Afraid to stain her dress, Josie had put several layers of Kleenex under her arms.

"Oh, Daddy," she said, touching his brow. "I know how uncomfortable this is for you. At least I get to be in short sleeves."

"Don't worry, *mija*. I'm fine. I only have to do this once for each of you." He was wearing the tuxedo he had bought for his own wedding. Monica had let out the waist and Josie thought it suited him just fine.

Her engagement had lasted for so long that she was caught off guard by Sancho's words. They made Time beyond her wedding day as blinding as the sunlight streaming down on them through the open doors. Her heart was pounding fiercely and she asked for a glass of water. Serena brought it to her in a paper cup.

"Are you all right?" her sister asked. Scanning Josie's face, Serena had no time to say anything before she was summoned to start her walk down the aisle.

"Well, are you?" her father asked. He touched her arm gently.

"Yes, yes. It's the heat," Josie said and swallowed hard. "Why doesn't Modesta hurry up? It will be cooler inside." She spilled some of the water on the front of her dress and saw herself melting into the mosaic tiles beneath her. She laughed. "Oh, Daddy. I guess I am nervous after all."

Sancho looked at his daughter with tears in his eyes and with what she called his cat smile. "We all were, *querida.* Just remember that weddings and funerals have one thing in common. They're for everybody else but the people who have to go through them." He kissed her on the cheek and eyelids.

Modesta began to play the bridal march. "Are you ready?" he asked her.

The knocking at her chest was unbearable. Ready for what? To be joined forever, even beyond the grave, to a creature who in that terrifying moment Josie felt she hardly knew? Were all brides this frightened? Was she the one, joyless exception?

She fought against burping and wished she had not drunk the lukewarm water. Her mouth tasted like the paper cup and her ribs ached. The rest of her seemed unreal and doll-like, weighed down by the heaviness of her gown.

Before them, the main doors were opened wide by unseen forces. Josie was aware of the desert light slicing at her neck through the veil and of the strong grip of Sancho's gloved hand at her elbow guiding her through the threshold.

"Don't worry," she heard him say above the din of the organ. For the bride's walk down the aisle, Modesta let out all the stops. "Nobody's ever ready. We just get used to it after a while."

His words slapped her in the face and rescued her from the hysterical thought that in two hours, nothing would ever be hers alone again. Feeling the dryness at her back, Josie saw herself in the wilderness hunting and fishing with her father. Oh, Daddy, turn me into a tree.

"Take a breath," Sancho told her. "Smile, *mija*. Show everyone how beautiful you are."

Josie let herself burp and started smiling halfway down the aisle. Her heart stopped racing in opposite directions, and she began to breathe naturally. She was on her way to forever.

"Good girl," Sancho said. "Let's get this part over with so we can dance."

The spray of stephanotis in her hand stopped quivering. "I'm a woman," Josie said more to herself than to her father. "I'm not afraid of anything."

xii

Until the doors were closed behind them, Miguel Chico and the rest of the wedding party at the altar railing saw Josie and Sancho as shadows emerging from the desert light. Across from him the jerky movements of Yerma's bouquet caught his eye. From childhood, their delicate cousin was given to fainting, and he wondered who was going to catch her and keep her from cracking her head on the marble floor. Yerma's face was turned away from the glare and her eyelids were flickering in time to the music.

"She'll never make it," he said to Rudy. He was moving his shoulders up and down.

"Me either. This monkey suit is itching me to death. Why don't they close the damn doors? They're letting the heat in." At that instant, the doors were shut. "Hey, Mickie, a miracle. I caused a miracle."

Modesta struck another wrong note as Josie floated by the statue of the Little Flower. Miguel Chico half expected the lipstick-red roses to melt in protest.

Josie was smiling away as if they were all part of a joke being played on them. At last, father and bride reached the foot of the altar. The family, the guests and wedding party—all saw Sancho Salazar lift the veil away from her face and over her head. Behind her, Eduviges smoothed the gauzy white material around Josie's shoulders and returned to her place in the front pew.

When she walked by him, Josie glanced wickedly at Miguel Chico. He saw that her eyes were darker than usual and felt his heart shrivel at the loss of their childhood.

The couple exchanged vows in English and Spanish, after which Father Vandermeer celebrated the traditional mass in Latin. Josie saw, every time she turned to look at her, that her mother was pleased by the length of the ceremony. Her own moods in those two hours shifted like clouds from happiness to indifference to trepidation and back again in a round that reminded her of saying the rosary. Now and then, her eyes met Harold's with affection.

Most everyone on the Angel side of the church received communion, during which Modesta played a lugubrious "Ave Maria" almost ten times before the last communicant returned to his pew. The fifth time, Josie began singing along, correcting the false notes and substituting the words of popular songs to keep from thinking about the ache in the small of her back. Behind her, she heard Serena humming with her.

In a departure from tradition, which her mother read as symbolic later and did not like from the beginning, Josie and Harold were kneeling across from each other instead of side by side. Josie wished he would smile or frown or do anything but remain so completely still. She wanted to know what a man felt when giving his life to another in such an irrevocable and public way. Except for an occasional elfin grin, his face remained relaxed and impassive.

Only once during the preparations had Josie seen his face charged with emotion. At the rehearsal, Harold and his brother had quarreled about the lilac-colored tuxedos.

"I am not putting that on to please anybody," Gregory said.

"Oh, Greg, what difference does it make? Can't you ever have any fun?" Harold had his hands on his brother's shoulders.

"Weddings are serious," Gregory said, looking at

Josie, and he walked out before the others noticed anything was the matter. Harold followed him to the car.

When he returned, his face was splotchy and his mouth swollen as if he had been in a fist fight. Josie kissed him gently.

"Did he hit you?"

"No. I'll tell you later. We need to find someone else to take his place." There was blood on his handkerchief.

They called Ofelia's husband from the rectory and asked him to be the best man. There was just enough time to alter the suit to fit him. Henry had grown stouter in the early years of his marriage to Ofelia and his jolly ways delighted the younger members of the family. "I'll do it," he said. "I've always wanted to dress up like a purple penguin."

And that is what her brother-in-law became, round and jovial and ready to fuss like a best man. She saw that the knees of Harold's trousers were now damp with perspiration and that Rudy was having a hard time keeping his eyes open.

At the signal, the couple stood and joined hands in front of Father Vandermeer for the final blessing. Josie was barely aware of Serena leaning over to pick up something from the train of her dress. Harold's face touched hers and when they turned toward the people, more Kleenex fell out of Josie's sleeves. They laughed all the way up the aisle and out of the Cathedral.

Behind them, Miguel Chico did not see the tissues escaping from under Josie's arms. His eyes were on Yerma, swaying like a pale-colored dahlia in a dry wind. "Rudy," he whispered, "will you please catch her before she hits the ground?"

Rudy did and escorted her out as if she were an invalid. Yerma fainted again at the reception after a few sips from a glass of pink champagne.

When the newlyweds arrived at the Daughters of Mary Hall after the interminable photograph-taking session at Tony Canales Studio, the family and guests were lined up and eager to greet them. Before joining Harold at the head of the line, Josie went to the ladies' room and took off her stockings.

"Here, Serena. Give these to Mother."

To Harold, waiting for her, she said, "Welcome to the *familia feliz*. Good luck."

The newlyweds greeted all the Angels, their relatives by marriage, family friends and any of the children patient enough to wait in line to touch Josie's dress. Later, she counted more than two hundred signatures in the guest book.

The Chavezes and the Gonzalezes from the west side of the mountain were mingling with the Ramirezes, the Castros, and Garcias from the northeastern part of town. Some of the Salazars from the southside attended, laughing and talking to the Aguilars, who drove in from Juarez for the occasion. Seated at the same table, they were ignoring the Blancos from Las Cruces, New Mexico, because they considered them traitors to the homeland.

The Casillas and Tamayo families arrived from Nayarit and Los Mochis and were serenading them with bawdy songs that were making even Mama Chona laugh. Josie loved watching the old men and women, toothless and grinning away, stamp their feet and clap their hands and not always in time to the music.

Pepe Hernandez, who had lost his faith that Spring, and his sisters Consuelo and Emma, who prayed for him every day, flew in from Mexico City. They were comforting their nosy second cousin Salubria Lozano, who traveled by bus from Chihuahua with her latest companion, missed the mass at the Cathedral, and was weeping from heat and heartbreak in and out of his arms. Consuelo and Emma did not recognize him and dared not ask his name.

Even ancient Matilde Mora rolled in, strapped to her wheelchair, and offered them the half smile created years earlier when she went into the house from working in the cactus garden, swallowed down an entire glass of iced tea without taking a breath, and suffered a cerebral hemorrhage that paralyzed the right side of her body. She took Josie's fingers in her gnarled hand and put them to her lips.

Helping Matilde manage the wheelchair were the gorgeous Portillo twins, dressed tightly in red, strapless outfits that paid tribute to their current favorite Hollywood star. Staring at them from across the room, Tano Hinojosa, whose leg had been blown away in Korea, was going crazy because he could not make up his mind which of the two he desired more.

Josie and Harold greeted the twins' saintly mother, Margie, as she made the sign of the cross in the direction of their foreheads before hugging them. Her rake of a husband, Alberto, whose thick head of gray hair made him look like a patriarch, kissed Josie on the mouth just long enough to embarrass her.

Aunt Trini, forever late, followed them and said, "I'm so happy." She was cooling her moist, mumpy face with a paper fan from the Chinese market on Pershing Street. "I've just come from the doctor and he told me that I don't have cancer after all. I was so sure I did."

"I'm glad, Tia," Josie said and steered her on. Trini dropped the fan and bumped heads with Harold when they both bent down to retrieve it.

Mrs. Goodlow and her husband, Charlie, the only Anglos on the block who did not move out when families like Josie's started moving in, took her hands and told her once again what a good time Mexican people had. "You're always so happy," the old lady said.

"Shall we tell her why?" Josie said in an aside to Serena.

"I'm having a good time," her sister answered.

"Of course you are," Josie said and found herself gasping for breath in Kiko Haddad's bear hug. "Why did you get married?" he said into her ear. "You could have had me anytime."

"I didn't want you anytime," Josie said loudly enough for Harold to hear. "Meet my husband, you nut." She squeezed Kiko's arm with affection.

Several of her Syrian and Jewish friends from high school came to her wedding. The Haddads, Abrahams, and Ekerys brought sumptuous gifts of fabric embroidered by Lucy Katchadourian. The Schwartzes and the Shapiros paid for several place settings of silver in her pattern on display at Feder's Jewelers. The Reigel sisters, whose father had helped many families escape from the Holocaust and settle on the border, gave them an automatic toaster from the Popular.

"Did you hear about Doris Hansen?" Mimi Reigel asked after making two little popping noises with her pixie face at Josie's cheeks. "She's pregnant and has run away from home. Nobody knows where she is." She looked at Josie as if she knew and was just waiting to be told.

Josie had no time to respond. Doctor Aguilera's Swing Band was ready for the newlyweds to begin the dancing. The last of the children in line helped Josie pick up her train and watched Harold lead her to the middle of the floor. Their gleaming eyes transformed her into a magical creature. She was a bride.

The saxophones started playing "The Anniversary Waltz" and everyone applauded as the couple glided by them around the hall. After that, Josie danced with her father-in-law while Harold danced with her mother. Then she found herself in Sancho's arms, surrounded by more dancers shuffling happily by to the Mexican polka blaring out of the Swing Band trumpets.

"Are you having a good time, *mija?*" her father asked.

"Yes," she said, barely hanging on to her train as he twirled her about. "And if I could take this damn dress off, I'd dance with everyone."

"You look very pretty," Sancho said.

"Don't, Daddy, or I shall cry."

She even danced with Salubria Lozano's companion. "His name is Jaime Schultz and he's from Veracruz," she told Serena. "My feet are killing me."

"Is that all? What else did he say?"

"God only knows where Salubria found him, he must be twenty years old. He says they met coming out of a Maria Felix movie at the same time with tears in their eyes. From that moment, his heart no longer belonged to him and he was overwhelmed with joy, for he had been ready to kill himself that very day for want of love in his life."

"How romantic!" Serena said, believing every word.

"Too romantic. I wonder what he wants from her? Look at the poor dear." A little tipsy, Salubria was dancing and flirting with their uncle Manuel, the skirt of her purple dress rising dangerously above her powdered knees. They saw Jaime Schultz watching the couple with sad, caramel-colored eyes, his handsome lower lip quivering with jealousy.

"He's the kind who kills for love," Josie said.

"Now who's being romantic? He's just a lovesick kid, that's all."

"Well, if you ever see me look like that, pinch me. Why don't you go get Aunt Sally to dance with him. She'll get the truth out of him."

"What truth?" Harold asked and startled Josie.

"You scared me. You always just appear or disappear, Harold. It's not fair. Look at him, Serena. Isn't he wonderful?" His face glowed.

Serena agreed that he was and left them to complete their duties as bride and groom. Protected by air conditioning from the heat of the late afternoon, Josie and Harold cut into the four-tiered wedding cake from the Aracataca Bakery. Following a custom Josie thought foolish, she placed a piece of cake in Harold's mouth and he in hers while flashbulbs recorded the moment for the family chronicles. They sipped champagne from silver-plated goblets loaned to them by Tia Cuca for the occasion, kissed again for the cameras, and walked through the crowd to special dressing rooms to change into their traveling clothes.

Her mother and sisters were waiting to help her. Josie braced herself. "Get this thing off me," she said, stepping out of her shoes and taking the pins out of her hair.

"Your father sold his car to pay for it and the wedding, Josefa. You could be a little more grateful."

"Mother, let's not quarrel. The wedding was what you wanted. I would have gladly eloped. So don't start telling me how I should feel. You knew from the beginning."

Ofelia and Serena pulled the dress over her head and gasped when they saw that their little sister was stark naked.

"I don't care," Josie said. "It was too hot."

Serena smiled at the beauty of her sister's figure and skin. Face averted, Ofelia handed Josie the first undergarments she found in the valise.

"I'm not wearing them. I'm wearing slacks and that blouse."

"You are a little savage," her mother said. "Thank God I kept Mama Chona from being in here while you changed."

"I'm all flesh, Mother. There aren't going to be any immaculate conceptions in my family."

"Josefa, *por favor*. Don't blaspheme on your wedding day."

Josie flattened the collar of her blouse and leaned over to brush her hair. "I'll go ask Henry if Harold is ready," Ofelia said, and walked out of the room.

Serena adjusted a thin, gold-colored chain around Josie's neck. Her back to them, Eduviges was carefully placing tissue paper in the folds of the wedding gown.

"What's this?" Josie asked.

"Just a chain. You don't have to wear it if you don't want."

"I'm afraid to ask what the medal is." Her throat was aching.

"It's *la Virgen* of you know what. Gobble, gobble."

"Oh, Serena," Josie said and hugged her sister close.

"Hug your mother," Serena said into her ear.

"Sure," she said out loud. "Mother, turn around. Serena wants me to hug you."

Eduviges straightened her shoulders and accepted Josie's embrace. Her lips were set tightly over her teeth and the lids above her dry eyes were as thick and heavy as an archangel's.

"Smile, Mother. Aren't you glad to be rid of me?"

Eduviges' hand moved in a flutter before her face and she went back to folding the dress. Serena's tears flowed freely and her nose ran unchecked. Unable to swallow, Josie fought an impulse to rush out of the room.

"You'd think I was going to my funeral," Josie said.

Serena laughed and wiped her nose with the sleeve of her dress. She hugged Josie again.

"Serena, how many times have I told you to use a handkerchief?"

"Oh, Mother, there's no one like you. I'm going to find Harold. Serena, please bring the valise, I've got my carrying case. Give me the bouquet."

Harold was ready and waiting for her in the small lobby of the Hall. Some of the guests were slow-dancing, and the children were pushing Matilde's wheelchair back and forth in time to the music. She was sound asleep despite the birdlike twittering around her. Her cousin Gabriel, just completing his first year in the seminary, was with them. He smiled and waved to her. Josie waved back on her way toward Harold.

He and Henry were exchanging stories with the older male guests. Harold nodded politely and grinned when the others burst into loud peals of laughter. Having just left a room of women, Josie was struck by the strangeness of men. Her mother would have thought them all Indians. Josie's heart leaped toward them.

"Are they telling you stories about a virgin's first night?" she said to Harold. The men fell silent, instantly modest in her presence. "Don't stop. I want to hear them, too," she said.

"Later," Harold said, looking at her with clear eyes. "Right now, the virgins are waiting for you to toss the bouquet."

Josie turned toward them. The young women gathered in a bunch around her and then moved away in a bunch, their reedy arms stretched out and ready to snatch at the bouquet that arced toward them, sailed wide to the left, and fell to the floor. In the silence that followed, superstition hung dustily in the air until Serena picked up the flowers and put them back into Josie's hands.

"Try again, sister," she said with a smile and the atmosphere lightened. Yerma caught the bouquet and fainted for the third time that day.

Seated by the door in what Josie thought of as her Mother Superior role, Mama Chona was waiting to give her granddaughter a final blessing. Mema and Jesus Maria were by her side, eyes filled with wonder and experience. Despite the conventional life her aunt led, Josie knew that Jesus Maria was the real dreamer in the family. It was their aunt Mema who taught them all about the world by living in it.

"Get me through the rest of this," she said to Harold and walked slowly toward the older women. She leaned down to give Mama Chona a furtive kiss on the brow.

"Be good," her grandmother said in Spanish and in the flat, monumental tone she used for important occasions. "Offer your children to God, Josefa." Her eyes were gentle and astonished Josie. "Pray to the Little Flower."

"Yes, Mama Chona, I promise," she said, inhaling the smells of her childhood. Quickly, she kissed her aunts and took Harold's arm. "Take me away from here."

The heat and light struck them like gongs. After her eyes adjusted to the brightness, she saw her father standing to one side of the door. He approached and embraced her without a word.

"I'm going fishing, Daddy," she said, not trusting herself to look at him. He was unable to speak.

"Good-bye, cousin," she said gaily to Miguel Chico a few steps below. "I'll give you all the gory details when I get back."

Hand in hand, she and Harold ran down the remaining stairs to the car toasting like a big red *chile*

by the curb. The crowd pelted them with rice. When
the first grains fell on her face and hair, Josie looked
at Serena in surprise and said, "Oh, my God! I'm
married!"

She waved and leaned her head out of the window for as long as she could see the children running
after them down Myrtle Street. Along with the
strange sound of her voice calling out good-bye,
Josie heard the tin cans clank dully against the hot,
black pavement and the fluttering of the white crepe
paper flowers strung across the vermilion hood of
Harold's Plymouth.

"I can hardly wait to tell our children about
today," Josie said, shading her eyes with her hand to
protect them from the glare of the sun now leaving
the earth. Behind dark glasses, Harold let her chatter
away and drove north through the town toward the
Alamogordo highway.

Looking after them through the tops of the
drooping mimosa and Chinese elm trees, Miguel
Chico felt he was inside a heart on fire with joy and
sorrow. Rice stuck to his hands. A few paces away,
he heard Josie's father sobbing like a child. Sancho's
arms were draped puppet-fashion over his aunt's
delicate shoulders and Miguel Chico was overwhelmed by fear and pity at the sound of his uncle's
weeping.

"Don't cry, Sancho. Don't cry," Eduviges said to
him softly in Spanish and caressed the tears away
from his face. "She'll be back. You'll see."

xiii

Josie and her sisters had been born during the Great Depression and as far as she was concerned, Del Sapo, Texas, was still in it when she returned to the desert from California after almost ten years of marriage.

In a heat wave that reminded Josie of her wedding day, she arrived at her mother's doorstep with her daughters Hanna and Rebecca in hand and no husband in sight. Josie was to be the only divorced woman in the Angel family and, as she made it a point to say at gatherings in that first year, "Several removes from the purity of the Little Flower. I've turned into a cactus. Watch out."

On the way back, questions about her life and her sisters' lives appeared like mirages in the road, real enough from a distance, becoming nothing when she drove through them. How was she going to keep her girls from rushing headlong into such ghostly places without stifling them with her love and care? Does one generation learn from another? Why is it the women who always have to clean the toilet bowls and change the diapers? Would she marry again? How were the three of them going to live on her salary?

When, as a child, Josie had asked the impossible questions, Mama Chona told her to pray to her patron saint for guidance. Saint Joseph! From the start, Josie thought him a terrible bore, a background figure who fell out of the main story unnoticed, necessary only once—to save the child from a hateful king's wrath. What good was he after that? A ridiculous character!

Like me, she thought, halfway to Del Sapo. Joseph, Mary didn't need you any more than Harold needed me. And you weren't even the father of her child, according to Holy Mother the Church. What a dope!

She felt sorry for him and angry with herself. Why didn't you stay in Egypt, Joseph? Why am I going back to the desert? What will my girls find there? Josie considered her sisters.

Ofelia had married six months after her high school graduation. That was the custom among young women in the late forties and early fifties, Mexican or Anglo. Ofelia was smart enough to have gone on to college, even if the local institution was devoted mainly to mining and engineering. But Mexican American girls from lower middle-class families were not expected to continue with their education, no matter how gifted or intelligent. They were expected to marry and begin having children as soon as possible. This was seen as obeying natural law and the dictates of the Church. Ofelia had done both in her perfect way.

She married a decent man of Anglo-Mexican

background. He had a good paying job in the utility company of the town where the noise in his department was such that he lost most of his hearing by the time his second child was born. Despite their Anglo surname, Ofelia brought up her children to follow Mama Chona's rules. After all, they were Angels and must learn the family's traditions.

Serena, small and robust and perfectly suited to her job as a P.E. teacher in the same high school her parents and cousins had attended, did earn a master's degree at Texas Western. Josie remembered how when she was twenty, Serena had almost married a tall, thin, fair-haired basketball player and champion swimmer who was worshiped by the town. The engagement lasted three weeks and was broken off amid tears of dismay and frustration, followed by a silence that left the younger members of the family puzzled and without a sports hero.

"It's because he was Anglo, right?" Josie had said to her sister.

"I don't want to talk about it," Serena said, and she didn't, not even to Josie.

Several years later, Serena and Mary Margaret Ryan, an algebra teacher from Boston, moved into an apartment in central Del Sapo. Their neighbors were elderly people, mostly widows living out their last days in the desert. Serena and Mary Margaret attended daily mass along with the relatives and friends too feeble to drive themselves to the Cathedral, and were regarded by the family and others as angels of mercy. They had been together twelve years when Josie came back from California with Hanna and Rebecca.

"So you turned into a nun after all," Josie kidded her sister. Serena helped them find and move into a small, two-bedroom house by Ascarate Lake within three months of their arrival.

"Not quite," Serena said. "I love my beer. And I'm hooked on bowling." The sisters laughed.

Everyone loved Serena. Her good spirits, like her laugh, were infectious, even among her cynically minded and chronically depressed relatives—Josie and their cousin Miguel Chico, in particular. Serena's acts of generosity placated her mother's fears and held at bay the judgment of those Angels who were suspicious about the erotic lives of others because their own were so dull.

Serena served people gladly and with a sincerity of heart that kept anyone from questioning her life too closely—not that any family member would do that directly—or from making demands that would drive her and Mary Margaret away from the town and into "God knows what abyss?" as Eduviges, who believed in abysses, said to her husband. Josie saw how Serena's acts of charity protected her and forgave her sister the duplicity of her life. She knew the truth and was afraid for Serena.

"How's your abyss?" Josie asked Serena with a knowing smile now and then when they were alone.

"Wonderful. You ought to plunge in."

"No, thanks. I don't want to deal with anyone else's ego ever again. Mine is definitely enough
for me."

"Chicken. You're still gorgeous. Get out there
and show it, girl."

"I'm too tired." She was working overtime so that
she would not have to ask her father to help pay for
the girls' schooling.

"You sound like Meg. All she wants to do is play
golf and sleep on our days off. You two are just alike.
I swear you could both sleep through tornadoes."
Serena spoke with some caution, for Josie and Meg
did not get along. She had given up on her attempts
to get them to be friends. The women remained cool
and distant toward each other, even in Serena's presence.

This time, Josie laughed and said, "I was just
seeing myself as an Indian abyss watching television.
I guess that's what I've become. Don't tell Mother."

Josie knew that what she was in the family's eyes
was a sinner. Not one of her relatives—not even her
mother—would have called her that to her face, for
they were good Catholic people and needed media-
tors to guard them from truths and keep them comfortable. Instead, some of the Angels let her know
her place by shifting the atmosphere away from the
tropical every time she, the fallen woman, arrived at
a gathering of the tribe.

"I can feel their coldness," Josie said to Serena. "I
don't care what you say."

"You're nuts," her sister replied. "They all love you."

"I know some of them do," Josie said. "It's how that bothers me. Serena, you are so naïve. You think of love as always being good. Sometimes, it destroys people."

"Not if it's real love. Now I know you're crazy. What are you reading these days? Whatever it is, it's wrong."

Serena preferred to blame outsiders for Josie's views on the Church and the family, but in her heart she knew that Josie believed what she said about herself and others. She saw that her younger sister had armed herself against shame, but that she was helpless before the forces that changed atmospheres.

In the early years of her divorce, Josie and Serena watched their Anglo women friends leave husbands right and left, go to court for alimony and child support, and find new careers and other men. The sisters nursed several of the wounded in the first painful months of separation, loss, and ugly revelations.

"I think Colette is doing exactly the right thing. I would have left that son of a bitch ages ago. Or killed him when I found out he had been doing those things to my daughters." Josie aimed these words at her mother's back. Eduviges was cooking lunch for her and Serena.

"Isn't it awful?" Serena said. "Who would have thought that quiet, mousy guy was such a snake?"

She sneezed. "Just thinking about it gives me an allergy attack. And he's a philosophy professor, too. I don't get it."

Josie laughed. "He's an Anglo, Serena. They can do anything they want, remember?" She glanced again at her mother. She was pan-frying the boquilla bass Sancho had caught that weekend. The smell of burning butter and blackened fish filled the room like incense.

Eduviges remained silent and sat down to bone the bass at the table. "Anglos can do anything they want," their mother was fond of telling them. "And look what happens to them, especially the women. They end up paying psychiatrists and taking pills or drinking themselves to death."

This time, handing Josie her plate, she said, "Your little girlfriends who think they're so independent are on their way to leading empty lives with no family to keep them company and care for them in their old age. If that's what freedom amounts to, they can have it. Here, Serena, I made these *nopalitos* for you. I put onion and tomato in the sauce this time."

"Oh, I see," Josie said, ignoring Serena's eyes. They were telling her to drop the subject. "She's supposed to stay with a husband who has been molesting her children. Is that right, Mother?" She cut into the fish with her fork as if it were a piece of red meat.

"The *nopales* are delicious, Ma," Serena said.

"Where did you get them? Josie, taste them." She offered the bowl to her sister.

"I don't want any. I hate cactus. Is there any *chile*? This fish needs some flavoring worthy of it." She waited for Eduviges to tell her that she drowned all her cooking in *salsa* and ruined it.

"I'll get you some. It's in the fridge," Serena said and rose from the table.

"Is that right, Mother?" Josie asked again and spooned the hot sauce generously onto everything on her plate.

"If Colette married in the Church, she married for life," Eduviges said in Spanish. "God fits the back to the burden."

"Anybody want a tortilla? I'll warm some up," Serena said. She held one like a halo above and behind their mother's head in an attempt to distract Josie.

"What makes you so sure God cares, Mother?" Josie knew that her insistent tone wore down her mother's patience.

"I'm going to Michelle you, if you don't stop," Serena whispered.

Eduviges looked into Josie's Apache eyes. "I'm sure," she said again in Spanish to make her words more convincing. "Haven't you learned anything?"

What her first years as a divorcée had taught Josie was that she was special, not in a good way, but as an example to the younger generation of what happens when one does not obey the laws of nature and Rome. "There are no prodigal daughters," she said to

Serena after a family party she had attended unaccompanied by her mother or sisters.

"I don't know what you're talking about," Serena said.

"Never mind," Josie said. "No one in this family ever understands what I say or feel."

"Oh, Josie, give them a chance to get used to having you back in Del Sapo. You can't expect to have them adjust overnight. They will. You'll see."

"They're all so polite, it kills me. I know what most of them are thinking. I can feel the knives in my back every time I walk away."

"Sounds more like you're feeling guilt," Serena said. "That, too, will go away. Give yourself a chance. I'm so glad you came back with the girls. They are beautiful. Surely, you can see how much Mother and Daddy love them."

"Then why did she tell me we would all end up on the street without a husband or father to protect us? How can she say such things to me? Am I made of plastic?"

"You know how Mother is, Josie. She didn't mean it the way you took it. She cares about you and the girls. Divorce is one of those things she was taught to be scared of. She can't help it."

"Well, I'm scared of it, too, but I don't act like she does about it."

"Forgive and forget, sister. Get on with your own life and stop worrying about what anybody thinks," Serena said.

"You forgive and forget. You're the Catholic, remember? I'm a woman with two kids to worry about."

For a while after her return, Josie even considered seducing a younger second cousin or nephew right under her mother's nose so that she could be like one of her favorite characters in *The Charterhouse of Parma*. But Ofelia's children were all girls and Serena was beyond childbearing. There were no nephews handy and the rest of the male children in the younger generation were too young and uninteresting for her to bother.

The truth was that she was tired of thinking about men and the silly ways women had to behave in order to find and keep them. Much to the family's and her daughters' amusement, she began falling asleep at odd times and places, sometimes even in the middle of a phone conversation with Serena.

Later, Josie awoke wondering why she was under a comforter and still talking into a telephone that had found its own way back to the stand in the hallway. Hanna's head floated above the arm of the sofa and told her in a giggly way that she had dropped off and that it was time for her to get up and go to bed.

"You sure have gotten lazy," her uncle Miguel Grande said to her in that joking way that set Josie's teeth on edge. Though he looked more like her aunt Mema than Eduviges, his tone was like her mother's. "If I were your age, I'd be running around enjoying it instead of passing out everywhere." He enjoyed pushing the younger generation around.

"I do not pass out everywhere," Josie said casually. "And from what I hear, you're still running around. And at your age, Uncle. Shame on you."

"Well, I don't think there's much he can do," his wife Juanita said. "His knees won't let him. Those days are gone." Now that it was over, Josie marveled at the way her aunt spoke so freely about Miguel Grande's long affair with her best friend Lola.

"For me, too," Josie said, and instead of becoming a wicked, sensual aunt in a French novel, she turned into a sleeping desert princess cursed by a witch who made certain there was no prince in or around Del Sapo, Texas, to wake her with a kiss one fine, fall morning. Autumn was Josie's favorite season.

"Stay for dinner. Come on, eat with us," her aunt said genuinely.

"No, Tia. I have to stop by grandmother's with the groceries. I wonder who she'll think I am this time?"

When Josie had returned to the family, her mother, aunts, and uncles agreed among themselves not to mention the failure of her marriage in Mama Chona's presence. By then, the old woman was sliding into the gray well of senility and probably would not have known about what or whom they were speaking. Still, the Angels wanted to take no chances, and they gave Josie orders to keep quiet about the divorce, just in case she caught Mama Chona in a moment of lucidity, told her the awful truth, and hurled her out of the well and into eternity.

"Of course I'm not going to tell her, Mother. What do you take me for? I'm not that insensitive. Anyway, I doubt that she will even recognize me."

"Yes she will, Josefa."

She looked at her mother and saw that Eduviges believed what she was saying. Josie smiled. Neither dementia nor death could touch the Angels. How they were to enter the afterlife they were so crazy to reach was beyond logic and Josie.

"And don't look at me that way," Eduviges said. "Just do what we ask, please. There's no need for her to know. She's so fragile now."

"You mean frail, Mother. Mama Chona has never been fragile."

"Let's not argue, Josefa. Keep quiet for your father's sake if not for mine and the family's." Eduviges' arms were bent at the elbow, palms up, as if inviting an embrace. The women did not move.

Josie did as she was told, but after Mama Chona's death, she flaunted her state outside the realm of grace and made at least one scandalous statement about religion at all family occasions. These delighted her father when he heard about them.

In the privacy of the garage he had converted into a den for himself, Sancho looked at the old photographs of his daughters on the wall. His wife had framed and arranged them chronologically, a row for each child. Ofelia was smiling through life and he was grateful for that. Despite her name, Serena looked uncomfortable in all but one of the photos, ready to leap through the glass and into the world.

Only Josie, unsmiling, stared at him and everything beyond him with deep, defiant eyes so dark he could not make out their pupils. More than once after her return, sitting alone and enjoying the cigars he was not allowed to smoke in the main part of the house, Sancho felt Josie was the son he never had. His pity and love for her pierced through the whitish-blue screen of smoke between him and the wall.

"Poor child," he said.

xiv

On his first visit to Paris in the early seventies, Miguel Chico sent Josie a copy of a postcard he found in a sidewalk stall by the river. He was alone on that drunken, guilt-ridden walk along the Seine with the desert very much on his mind. The old postcard from the twenties made him laugh and broke into his sour mood.

It was a black-and-white photograph of a naked flapper tied to a huge cross by thick and shiny ropes that covered her groin. Her breasts were bare and perfectly shaped. Beneath bobbed hair, the young woman's face was ecstatic.

Dear Cousin,

    I have found our Saint Wretched at last! As soon as she's through gasping, she's climbing down to dance the twist till dawn at the local disco. It's called Le (French) Club (English).

Love,

Sor Juana de la Cruz

Josie's response was waiting for him when he returned to California.

Querido primo—

    I want you to know that I laughed till my stockings fell down when Saint Wretched arrived from gay Paree. She's hanging on my refrigerator door and I worship her now more than ever.

Love from me and the girls,

Anna K.

Will you be in Del Sapo for Christmas?

The Angel family had been gathering for midnight mass at Santa Lucia ever since Miguel Chico's brother Gabriel had been appointed parish priest there by the bishop. After the Christmas Eve ritual, which began at seven and ended at nine o'clock, the family got together for a feast at Ricardo Angel's home. His wife, Alicia, spent the first three weeks of December preparing for it.

On a visit to Del Sapo for the holidays, Miguel Chico was in his cups. All Christmases were beginning to melt into each other for him like the ice cubes in his drink.

"What year is this?" he asked Josie.

"What do you mean what year is this? Cousin, I'm worried about you." She laughed.

"I mean, how many years have we been going to Santa Lucia and to Ricardo and Alicia's? They're all the same to me. Only this time I feel we're going backward instead of into the future. I don't know what's happening to Time anymore."

"Nothing. You've had too much scotch, that's all."

"Me? I hardly touch the stuff."

The cousins were standing by Josie's car in the cold, clear desert night across the street from Juanita and Miguel Grande's house near Mesa Street. At dinner, Josie had told them she had offered her house for the post-midnight mass celebration, but that her mother and Ofelia had rejected the offer without even listening to her reasons.

"Alicia has been doing it for years. It's time for someone else to do it. She's not well and it's not fair that the burden falls on her every year," Josie said to her cousin, aunt, and uncle.

"But she loves doing it. I think it keeps her healthy," Miguel Chico's mother said and handed Josie a warm corn tortilla. Juanita had prepared *chile colorado*. She sat down to eat only after the rest were served and almost finished with their meal. Josie took the tortilla and salted it. She considered her aunt one of the true saints in the Angel family.

"Maybe. But I think Alicia is tired of it all and she needs to rest." Anyone who marries an Angel, male or female, has earned the rest, Josie wanted to add.

"How do you know she's tired of it all?" her uncle asked with great skepticism. Miguel Chico knew that his father thought Josie a troublemaker and a spoiled brat. Not waiting for her answer, Miguel Grande said simply, "I think you're nuts."

"That's what Mother thinks. God, you Angels stick together. What a family!" Josie looked at her cousin and asked, "How do you stand it?" She was serious.

"How about some coffee? I can make some," Juanita said.

"No thanks, Tia. I've got to get back to the house. I don't know if the girls have had dinner." Hanna and Rebecca attended a public school on the east side of town and were rehearsing for the annual Christmas concert.

"How are they?" Juanita asked. "I haven't seen them for a long time. Bring them with you next time."

"They wanted me out of the house after choir practice so they could wrap my presents without me there to supervise. I'll tell them you asked about them." Josie looked at Miguel Grande. "I don't care what you think, Uncle. I know Alicia's tired because she told me so."

"You're hearing things," he said with certainty.

"Ricardo himself told me at the Y today that Alicia has never felt better and that she's cooking more dishes than ever for the party." In Josie and Miguel Chico's generation, Ricardo was Miguel Grande's favorite. He enjoyed telling them that without all of their advantages, Ricardo had been more successful and was happier than they.

"I give up," Josie said and excused herself. She put on her coat in the living room, said good night to Juanita at the door, and spoke loudly toward the kitchen where her uncle was drinking his coffee, "Ask Ricardo about what the doctor told Alicia."

Juanita put a finger to her lips and shook her head. Josie hugged her. Miguel Chico got his jacket and walked her to the car. "Why don't they ever listen to me?" They were arm in arm against the sharpness of the wind.

Miguel Chico looked at his cousin with understanding and wondered why she hid her beauty by keeping herself just overweight enough to be noticeable and by not caring what her hair looked like most of the time. He wanted to see her as she was in high school—slender, smiling, and wearing dresses and bobby socks that did not measure up to her dark and lovely charms.

"Are you sure you're still not getting down on your knees to Saint Wretched? I don't believe all this hysteria about Christmas Eve is caused only by your mother and sister. Come on, cousin, confess. Where is the man in this picture of distraught, almost middle-aged womanhood?" Only he and Serena got away with talking to Josie in this way.

"God, Mickie, you know I have more problems with men than you do." She stopped. A gust of wind made the car shiver behind her.

"When Harold walked out on me and the children, I knew I had to be strong for them. I can see why he turned away from me, but I still don't understand how he could ignore Hanna and Rebecca. How can a father not care what happens to his children? I don't get it. And the one man I have gone out with in any serious way drinks too much and can't leave his mother. What's wrong with me? Tell me, Mickie. You know about men. Tell me."

He was looking away from her toward the silhouette of the mountain. From that part of town, it looked like the side of an elephant on its belly. In the silence that followed, Miguel Chico was embarrassed and Josie felt ashamed.

It was the first time she had stood in a nonjoking way so near the gate of his secret territory. Years earlier and without having to be told, she had understood that her cousin was a lover of men. Their camaraderie as sinners was born out of that intuitive and unspoken revelation. When she became the only divorced woman in the family, they grew even closer and glowed in each other's company when sitting in the living rooms and dens of their relatives.

After their uncle Felix was murdered in the mid-sixties and the newspapers had trampled through and exposed his hidden life, Eduviges had declared to them all, "I don't believe a word of it. There are no homosexuals."

"You mean there are no Lebanese ladies or Homersensuals in the whole world or just in Del Sapo, Mother?" Josie had spoken with sarcasm and a smile, using the terms she and her cousins had invented for Sodom and Gomorrah. Serena and Miguel Chico, sitting together on the sofa, had been too grief-stricken to join Josie in her taunts at death and Eduviges.

"I guess you're right after all, Mother," Josie had gone on, disappointed in her sister and cousin for not speaking out. "And not all the clapping in the world will bring Tinkerbell or Felix back to life."

"Please be quiet, Josie," Serena had told her. "You know what it's like in Del Sapo."

"I know that this stupid town is narrow-minded, religious in the worst of ways, and condones murder." She had walked out of her mother's house and wept for her uncle alone in Serena's car.

Later that awful week, she had persuaded her cousin JoEl, Felix's youngest child, to let her help him clean up the bloodstains in his father's '55 Chevrolet. She had been driven to her wedding in it.

"My father's not dead," JoEl had told her. "He's coming back."

"Of course he is, JoEl," Josie had said gently to him. The stain remover was not working and she was awed by the horror her uncle must have felt while being beaten to death.

"No one believes me, Josie," JoEl had said. "I know he's not dead."

Josie saw a different kind of denial at work in Miguel Chico, and it bothered her to watch it destroy him from within. In his last visits to the desert, she noticed that he was drinking too much and that the puffiness around his eyes was ruining his handsome face.

"I'm sorry, Mickie. As usual, I'm mad as hell with no one to talk to about it. You know how they deny any unladylike feeling." He was looking at her with kindness.

"I think my mother has finally gotten to me. After all these years and all the battles, I'm tired. I've lost and I hate it. And I especially hate it when they look at me like your father—as if I'm crazy. Even Serena has started staring at me in that way." There was no sarcasm in Josie's voice.

"Darling, this is getting very old," Miguel Chico said and put his arms around her. "You've got to stop playing the baby in your family. Your mother is not going to change. She's an Angel, remember? They were born perfect in that generation and know everything about life. Josie, you have the chance to change and I refuse to let you get boring on me. Come on, give it a rest. Who cares where we go for Christmas Eve? It's always the same."

Looking at her through the icy air, Miguel Chico

saw that she had not changed. The medieval atmosphere of Del Sapo was enough to drive any intelligent, sensitive person quite mad. Why had she returned so many years before? Why hadn't she stayed near him in California? In some places there at least, the world was not divided into the saints and the sinners.

"I care," she said. Josie leaned against the car. Miguel Chico's arms fell awkwardly against his jacket. He saw tears in the corners of her eyes, which made him uneasy. Not even in childhood had they allowed themselves to cry about anything when together. Tears, they had decided at a meeting of the Order, were only for the fake martyrs.

After a few moments of listening to the wind, Miguel Chico breathed deeply. The cold made his lungs feel like glass and his lips as dry as the sand collecting in small heaps along the gutters.

"Saint Wretched," Josie said into the wind. The tears were drying in her obsidian eyes. "I haven't thought about her since the girls started high school. Do you still have that wonderful card? I don't remember what I did with the copy you sent me. Probably Hanna or Rebecca took it." She was shivering.

"I have it and about a hundred copies of it. I'll send you one when I get back. Please don't make me worry about you, Josie. Of course, you're crazy. You always have been. Just like me."

He hugged her again and felt powerless to melt the coldness in her heart. Several tumbleweeds somersaulted down the street toward the mountain. He saw one get caught in the black wrought-iron fence that surrounded his parents' yard. In the dark, the pink of his mother's house was a deep lavender.

The wind from the east struck at his back. "It's going to snow," he said simply.

"It's not cold enough," Josie said.

"Wait and see. I want it to snow and snow. I love playing the Snow Queen. Hanna and Rebecca can be handmaidens. Tell them."

"You are a mess, cousin. What do I get to be?"

"You, my dear, will be the audience and the critics, as you are in life. Or, the director, but only if you let me wear whatever I want." He opened the car door for her with a bow. "Go home. I'm freezing my *nalgas* off."

"You haven't got any," Josie said and pinched him.

"Ouch! I won't be able to sit down for a week. Go!"

She got in the car and rolled down the window. "I guess we'll see you at Ricardo and Alicia's for the annual ritual of hypocrisy," she said. "Will you be at the mass before? I still haven't figured out why the bishop, that little toad, sent your brother out to the sticks. 'Poor Gabriel is in exile at Santa Lucia' is what Jesus Maria says to everybody. She's been saying it for eight years."

Miguel Chico moved as if he were being blown to the other side of the street. "Are you going to the mass?" Josie shouted. "I promised the girls I'd ask you."

"Yes! Yes!" he shouted back. He was waving as he ran up the steep driveway.

From inside the car, Josie saw his hands brushing against the brightness of the stars. She wondered where the moon was. She felt secure when it was around. Before she began warming up the engine, another rush of wind shook the car.

"I bet it does snow," she said and saw her breath disappear into the windshield. One of the backseat windows was slightly open. Leaning over to shut it, she heard Mama Chona's voice in the wind warning her about the darkness of the night.

"God," Josie said aloud. "Now, I'm not only talking to myself, I'm starting to hear voices from beyond the grave. I don't believe in an afterlife. Damn it, Mama Chona, the night is supposed to be dark."

She drove away and avoided looking into the rearview mirror all the way home.

BOOK TWO

Feliz Navidad

i

While waiting for Father Gabriel, the children of Santa Lucia liked talking about which had occurred first in the martyrdom of the maiden in whose honor the parish was established—the blinding or the violation.

"I mean, Chato, could she or couldn't she see what the Romans were doing to her?" one of the younger parishioners asked. Some of the seven-year-olds thought it was more horrible if she could see.

The virgin martyr's territory extended along the northern Rio Grande border between Texas and Mexico, which, in earlier days, was a dusty valley that depended on irrigation for its corn and cotton crops. In the sixties, the crops disappeared and she became the protectress of lower income housing divisions, a transformation that was more of a necessity than a miracle.

"It doesn't matter," Chato Medina answered

with authority and a touch of scorn. Among the most advanced in his catechism class, Chato had made his first communion four years earlier and was Father Gabriel's favorite altar boy.

One of his tasks every Saturday morning was to help train the younger children for their initial taste of the body and blood of Christ. Imitating the Roman soldiers' actions with his hands, Chato said, "The reason she was made a saint was because even after her eyes were brutally gouged out, she could still see." He had learned the word "brutally" that week in public school and was not yet tired of using it. Some of the children flinched and crinkled the corners of their eyes. A few looked to see how long Chato's fingernails were.

A statue of the blinded girl was placed on a pedestal to the left of the gymnasium door which served as the main entry for the congregation. Though quickly crafted by Manitas de Oro, the parish's resident sculptor who had finally been granted citizenship after many deportations, it was an impressive, life-sized, and very realistic rendering of a young maiden in her middle teens wearing what to one of the children seemed more like a nightgown than whatever Roman teenagers wore.

To others, the statue looked like a prettified version of Manitas' granddaughter Lucy. She was overweight and slightly cross-eyed as the children constantly reminded her when she came too near them. "At least my eyes are in my head," Lucy told them in self-defense.

The statue's empty eye sockets were gruesome. Manitas himself was almost blind, though he denied it and wore dark glasses to hide it. The community was not fooled, but went along with his pretense and watched him carefully so that he would not hurt himself on his daily walks through the neighborhood.

When asked by *la señora* Olguin and the members of the parish advisory committee, who did not like the statue, why he had made the face so realistic, Manitas replied, "So that people will really feel what that poor child suffered." Unconvinced, they told him they would have preferred a nicer, more clean-cut version of the "poor child," perhaps one that looked like the Little Flower of Jesus at the Cathedral.

Manitas ignored them. When in a bad mood, he told them he was an artist and not a maker of plastic tortillas. In his mind, this response made perfect sense. When in despair, he went into rages over shots of tequila with his best friend, Serapio Fuentes. "Those idiots would want Jesus on the cross to wear a suit from the Popular. They make me crazy, Serapio. They don't deserve to have an artist in their midst."

While working with the stone, Manitas had striven for an ethereal yet down-to-earth expression to shine through it, and he labored especially hard on the face and hands. The intricate patterns of the veins in the fingers were superbly and finely carved despite the rush to complete the statue on the date set by *la señora* Olguin for the dedication ceremonies.

"It's better than Michelangelo," Serapio said when Manitas invited him to a preview of his creation. He was especially impressed by the hands. One was at the maiden's breast and the other, palm wide open, was holding the ravaged eyeballs as if offering them to the world. "She is magnificent!" Serapio added.

Tugging at the seat of Manitas' pants, one of the children allowed to be at this early viewing asked him why the Romans had given them back to her. Chato Medina told them that the Romans ate parts of bodies and threw what they did not want to the lions, who were not particular about what they ate.

"They are symbols," Manitas said to this cherub of the block. The child, not understanding what a saint had to do with the percussion band in his grammar school class, nodded and pretended to follow Manitas' lecture on the maiden's suffering.

"People have to learn," the sculptor said in his most polished Spanish, "that we do not see with our physical eyes, that our eyeballs are only hard jelly and that we can only see what is true with our hearts. This poor girl knew that and when all the people in the world understand this great secret, then we will have paradise right here on earth. Until then, we are headed straight for the Devil where we will suffer more torments than this innocent child."

Manitas wiped the moisture from his face. His tears were for the beauty of his creation and not because of the cruelty the young girl had endured centuries earlier. Manitas was the kind of artist who remained dry-eyed before man's inhumanity to man. He preferred to outstare it or, in this instance, to let the eyeballs speak for themselves.

In the beginning, Manitas had also wanted to expose the virgin martyr's heart pierced by daggers and thorns, but the Bishop had told him the statue would look too much like the *Virgen de Guadalupe.* Manitas consoled himself by paying even more attention to the hands so that through them, he might give people a feeling for her spiritual beauty. He succeeded, though only Serapio and a few others in and out of the parish recognized Manitas' artistic accomplishment. For the most part, the parishioners were much more interested in the power to cure blindness and other less serious eye defects that the statue was said to possess.

ii

Twice, the maiden was taken from her pedestal. The first time, she was returned within twenty-four hours and no questions were asked of the woman who led Father Gabriel's housekeeper Doña Marina to the back of a pickup truck, where she saw it carelessly wrapped in cardboard and lying face up, the right hand making its grisly offering to the heavens. In her heart, Doña Marina wished the thieves had broken off that hand, for she found it offensive from the day she saw it. Most statues, artistic or not, did not appeal to her. She preferred trees.

For many years, Doña Marina had lived in a little room next to the kitchen of the ranch house that served as rectory for Father Gabriel and the many visiting priests from other parishes enamored of her cooking. Before then, the house had been the property of a rich Anglo rancher who had helped her get across the river and fallen in love with her delicious meals. He left the house to the Church when he died, with the stipulation that Doña Marina be allowed to live there as housekeeper and cook for as long as she wished.

Over the years, she grew stouter and her large, deep green eyes became even more beautiful. Whenever anyone in the parish forgot how to prepare a traditional dish or was missing an essential ingredient, they went to Doña Marina. *"Fideo* without *cilantro!* Impossible! Here, I have plenty. You can freeze it, you know. It doesn't look as good, but the flavor is all there."

The night of the loud knocking at her window, a cold night filled with stars she could almost reach up and touch from her bed, Doña Marina was soaking the makings for *pozole* and the entire house smelled of pork and corn. She was dreaming that the stars were falling into the stew, and it took her a few moments to realize there was a stranger at her window raving about the missing statue.

"I know it's gone," she said to the lunatic creature outside. In the darkness of her room, she could not tell if it was a man or a woman, but she did not want it to change its mind and run off to God knows where until she got a good look at it. "Wait right there," she said firmly. "I'll open the kitchen door."

Doña Marina made the sign of the cross several times from forehead to navel before she allowed a small, distraught woman into her kitchen. The stranger moved like an old lady. Doña Marina had seen many girls like her on the *calle* Mariscal in Juarez when, as a young girl, she had helped her mother cook for the patrons of one of the brothels very popular with the soldiers from the fort on the American side of the river. Doña Marina was ready to dismiss her until she saw the young woman's face.

"There were crucifixes in her eyes," she said to Father Gabriel later that day. "I didn't like her hair or the way her mouth moved when she tried to talk but her eyes kept burning my face." If Father Gabriel were not such a sound sleeper, Doña Marina was sure he would have been awakened by the moans of grief and gratitude the woman kept uttering.

She spoke like a deaf person and her oddly formed words were punctuated by Father Gabriel's snoring down the hall. Instantly, Doña Marina was transported into a frightful, unearthly land by the strangeness of these sounds in her kitchen. "It was like several devils had come into the house," she said to Manitas at their weekly poker game two days later. "I had to make certain no stars fell into my *pozole*. I asked her if she wanted some water. She said 'no' and began talking about the statue. Her eyes never blinked, Manitas, and the tears flowed without stopping until my spine started shivering."

Apparently, Doña Marina reported to Father Gabriel and Manitas, the woman had been raped by some scoundrel she had picked up in a bar on the American side of the river and, being a true child of the Church, she had not considered having an abortion when she found she was pregnant. The child was born blind and paralyzed from the neck down. "It was my punishment, it was my punishment," the woman said again and again, pounding her heart with a small and dirty fist. But now, she went on in her otherworldly voice, the little virgin saint had cured the child of its blindness so that it could see the people who loved it even if it could not move.

"I didn't believe the story, but I calmed her down by telling her that God does not punish anybody. She just got very, very quiet and stared in front of her as if I and the whole world had disappeared. It was scary. That child was pure suffering. I've never seen anything like it, Father, and I never want to again. It was a relief to get her out of my kitchen."

Doña Marina followed the silent woman to the truck, peered into the back and saw how the statue was wrapped. An old and a young man emerged from the darkness and, without saying a word to her, lifted the stone maiden out of the pickup and deposited her under an enormous Chinese elm tree that November had stripped of its leaves. The tree had grown in size and beauty despite the desert wind and all the construction around it since its sapling days when Doña Marina had nurtured and protected it. She loved that elm and thought it more magical than any statue, but she kept her mouth shut about that around the parish.

A pink and very cold dawn light was touching its top branches before Doña Marina realized that the young woman and the men with her were driving away. She could just make out the messages on either side of the truck's rear bumper: I AM A VIETNAM WAR VETERAN and PRAY THE ROSARY. "What cretins," she said to the tree and walked back into her kitchen where the bubbling and crackling noises of the *pozole* warmed and reassured her.

That afternoon, Father Gabriel and five young men of the parish carried and dragged the statue back to its rightful place. Manitas was called to examine it for damages. He found a small chip near the left elbow which he promised to repair immediately. Relieved and secure, the parish went about its business as usual.

The second time it disappeared, the statue was gone during the first two weeks of Advent and the community was beside itself with worry and a nagging feeling that if the statue were not returned, they would all wander through eternity without seeing Jesus and His Holy Mother. Children awoke at all hours of the night swearing that the maiden was in their room, eyeballs aflame, weeping and asking them to guard it against the Romans pursuing her relentlessly across Time and Space.

Constancia Rubio fell into a trance when she saw the statue in the clouds after a warm and gentle voice in her heart told her to look up and out of the window. "When I woke up, I smelled roses for the rest of the day."

Not to be outdone, la señora Olguin, who saw herself as the wisest and most saintly woman of the parish, said that the little virgin paid her a visit and sweetly asked her for a cup of hot chocolate. "You know," la señora said in a confidential tone to her neighbor Sonsa Trujillo, "I didn't know they drank chocolate in those old Roman times."

"Of course, señora," Sonsa replied. "Those Romans did everything they could to make themselves more potent so that they could act like barbarians to the Christians." Sonsa did not ask herself or la señora Olguin why the little saint would want to be more potent. She was used to her neighbor's hallucinations and had learned to stop asking questions about what la señora saw or did not see. Sonsa herself enjoyed whiskey more than chocolate.

In those days of the Second Disappearance, as it came to be known throughout the community, Manitas de Oro kept praying that the statue would appear at his door and he lit votive candles night and day in the hope of luring it into his house. He also used up the entire box of incense that Louie Mendoza had sent him from San Francisco during the hippie era. Manitas had been saving it for a special occasion, and even though the patchouli scent made his throat and head ache, he was convinced it would attract the virgin martyr.

Manitas wandered through those days wearing a bandana around his head and another to cover his nose and mouth and scared Lucy to death when, confusing her with his creation, he pounced on her at the door and threw her to the ground. The food she brought him for supper was ruined and before shutting her eyes tight, she saw a *birote* roll under the porch like a brown rabbit about to be slaughtered. Lucy herself had baked the little French breads that morning.

"It's you! It's you!" Manitas shouted until he saw who it was. By then, Lucy, in a half faint, had prepared herself for martyrdom at the hands of a half-crazed, lustful beast by crossing her arms on her chest and lying completely still as if already dead.

"Oh, my God," she heard her grandfather say. "I've killed Lucy." She opened her eyes and saw him kneeling and weeping beside her, using the bandanas to wipe his face and blow his nose.

"Stop crying, Grandpa. I'm all right," she said with some disappointment. Lucy wanted to be a saint.

After that incident, Manitas was like a man possessed and hardly ate or drank. When he slept, he dreamed that the teenage gangs of the neighborhood had kidnapped the little saint and were committing unspeakable acts in her presence that made her empty eye sockets weep bloody tears. Manitas awoke to find the pillows soaked through with his own perspiration and tears. "It's too horrible," he said again and again throughout the ordeal. Even Serapio and Doña Marina were unable to console him.

Finally, like a ghost, the statue returned as mysteriously as it had left them. This time, the people of the parish voted to put a wrought-iron grating around it and to chain it to the outside of the gymnasium wall. The chains crossed below the maiden's breast and were attached behind its back to an iron ring that was driven almost two feet into the concrete. The community wanted to make sure Santa Lucia did not vanish again and felt that only the most desperate sinner suffering from severe eye infection would be tempted to steal it.

• • •
iii

Jesus Maria Angel, wife of Manuel Chavez, did not belong to the parish of Santa Lucia and was not a believer in ordinary ghosts, human or artistic.

Proudly and with dignity, Jesus Maria believed in the Third Person of the Holy Trinity and wanted Him to remain invisible.

When she heard about the Second Disappearance in her nephew Gabriel's parish, she narrowed her lovely brown eyes and said, "Next, they'll be seeing the Virgin Mary in the tumbleweeds near Pecos, Texas. Why don't they leave the poor saints and martyrs alone?"

After Mama Chona's death, Jesus Maria became the spiritual leader of the Angel family and its standard of moral conduct, a role for which she thought herself well prepared by her lifelong faith in the Church. Having failed to satisfy her mother in the qualities of fidelity and obedience, Jesus Maria became the Cathedral's most devoted daughter. Only Modesta Gonzalez could claim to have attended as many masses and novenas as Jesus Maria.

When Mama Chona left her children to fend for themselves in the desert—and much to Jesus Maria's displeasure—the Angels began journeying across town to attend midnight mass on Christmas Eve at Santa Lucia's. Its location next to the border filled Jesus Maria with dread and sad, chaotic memories of her early life in Mexico.

"They may as well go back to Chihuahua," Jesus Maria said to her younger sister, Mema.

"Do you really think so, sister?" Mema said with indifference. She had lived in Juarez for many years before returning to care for Mama Chona in the last decade of her life. "I think it's a good thing for the

younger members of the family to begin to understand where they came from."

"Why? Where they came from does not care
about them and wouldn't lift a finger to help them."
Unlike her quiet, less intellectual sisters, Jesus Maria
spoke in a sophisticated border Spanish pronounced
the Mexican way. She enunciated every word perfectly and projected it outward without lisp or af-
fectation. She liked to think she meant what she said
despite the dramatic flourishes in her tone and
phrasing. People soon learned that the drama in her
voice was part of her nature and enjoyed her per-
formances. In another time and country, Jesus Maria
would have been a fine, if not splendid, actress in
roles demanding rage and pity.

"I cannot believe the Bishop would send Gabriel
out to the sticks like that. After all those years of
training, my nephew belongs in the Cathedral,"
Jesus Maria said. She was fully aware that Mema's
son Ricardo had just bought a house near Santa
Lucia.

Mema ignored her older sister's words spoken
with scorn the first time the family decided to pay
tribute to Gabriel for having been given his own
parish at last. It was made up of working-class families who lived in tract homes she knew Jesus Maria
found ghastly and emblematic of the moral decay
she saw everywhere. Ugly, beat-up cars rotting like
metal fruit on parched lawns and dirty sidewalks
were to her the manifestation of souls beyond re-

demption. To Mema, accustomed to life among the less privileged, the same cars symbolized the ingenuity of the poor.

"They have not even built the new church. We'll all be herded in like cattle into a gymnasium. I really do not understand what the Bishop thinks he's doing." Each year, for one reason or another, the funds set aside by the Bishop for the new church were reallocated and the people continued to sit on folding chairs and to kneel on the high school gymnasium floor. Built in haste before the school itself, the gymnasium was now its only relic because the city fathers had decided against spending any more money in a predominantly Mexican American area of the town.

"I am infinitely grateful that Mama Chona is no longer with us to bear such goings-on, Mema." Jesus Maria spoke as if their mother, like the Virgin Mary, had been assumed into heaven. "It will be like going to church in a wigwam. I am not an Indian."

Mema was unable to keep herself from laughing out loud at her sister's remarks. Pressing her lips together, Jesus Maria waited. One of her crosses was waiting for the rest of the world to see life as seriously as she did.

"And I simply cannot believe that the Bishop has consecrated and dedicated that part of town to an innocent and sweet virgin martyr like Santa Lucia. Wasn't it enough that the Romans brutalized and blinded her in the first century of our Lord's death?"

They heard her husband, Manuel, in the kitchen where he was washing the leavings of a day's work from his hands and forearms. No matter how hard he scrubbed with Bab-O and glycerine, the metallic and rubbery stains of the electrical wiring remained. Jesus Maria wrinkled her nose.

"God," she said towards the kitchen, "I'm glad that poor child can't see what the twentieth century is doing to her." She rose and signaled for Mema to follow her.

"The blind leading the blind," Manuel said, sitting down at the table to wait for his supper.

"What did you say, Manuel?"

He knew she had heard him. "Nothing," he said.

"I heard you. You and my happy sister will never understand anything about sanctity or self-sacrifice. Santa Lucia deserves more than a gymnasium filled with dust. I can just imagine the filth the river will deposit before her. Is that what she deserves for all her pain and suffering?" She peered into the pot and turned off the burner.

"I thought saints weren't supposed to care about material things." Manuel spoke in the logical tone that infuriated his wife and gave Mema a look of studied innocence.

"You know very well what I'm talking about, Manuel. You're just too stubborn and disrespectful to admit it."

He and Mema watched Jesus Maria stir the soup. She disliked all household chores, especially cooking. "I don't think Santa Lucia cares what people do to honor her, that's all," he said. "Is that a crime?" He was appealing to his sister-in-law, who knew enough to remain quiet.

Jesus Maria held the ladle above the pot like a baton. "No, it's not a crime. But the saints think about people more than you or Mema will ever understand." The baton became a ladle again and she served them the soup. Handing him the bowl, she said, "Grace is everywhere."

"Well, I think so, too," Manuel said. He tasted the soup. "Do you think she could heat up the soup a little more?"

He and Mema laughed. Jesus Maria ignored them and said once more in her most definite tone, "That poor, innocent child."

Manuel stared at his wife. He could not make up his mind whether he wanted to shake her or kiss her. The soup was lukewarm and oversalted.

"Eat before it gets cold," Jesus Maria said to them.

iv

"Now that's what I call real bondage and discipline," Jesus Maria's favorite nephew, Miguel Chico, said in her presence when he saw the statue of Santa

Lucia chained to the wall. It was the Angels' second gathering at his brother Gabriel's parish. Miguel Chico had missed the first because he was recovering at the university hospital from an operation for intestinal cancer and had decided to celebrate the holidays in California.

Though Jesus Maria did not care for the statue as a work of religious art, she found the remark very glib and disrespectful, perhaps even blasphemous. She also did not know exactly what he was talking about, but she sensed something indecent in the sound of his words.

When they were in high school, Jesus Maria had encouraged her nieces and nephews as well as her own children to study hard so that they could go away to college. She told them that if she had been born in another time and place, she, too, could have attended a university.

"We had to worry about having enough food on the table so that you could better yourselves and bring honor to the Angel family name," she said whenever they began criticizing family traditions or questioning the authority of the Church. By the time her grandchildren began their schooling, with Mama Chona so long in the grave, Jesus Maria was unable to keep heresy away from her family. "College was supposed to help you, not ruin you," she told them at every opportunity.

"Yes, Tia," they responded, smiling among themselves in that way that excluded her.

"Have respect," Jesus Maria said in response to Miguel Chico's coarse comment about the statue. "Or God will punish you." *Castigos de Dios*—God's punishments—was a much-used family phrase when misfortune visited any one of their homes.

The Angels were making their way through the Santa Lucia crowd, which smelled of tamales and a hint of *mezcal,* to sit in a special row of folding chairs reserved for them near the makeshift altar. The regular parishioners, Miguel Chico noticed, remained distant and respectful except for the few old ladies, their dark skin remarkably free of wrinkles, who greeted his mother, Juanita.

Gabriel had described a few of the more illustrious members of the parish to them, but Miguel Chico did not see anyone who looked like *la señora* Olguin or Manitas de Oro. After seeing the statue at the door, he wanted very much to meet the artist. The man escorting them to their seat introduced himself as Chato Medina's father.

Behind Mr. Medina, Miguel Chico took his aunt's arm and guided her down the center aisle. Once again, he was captured by her beauty and youthfulness. Throughout her life, Jesus Maria appeared twenty years younger than she was.

"I'm sorry, Tia," he said to her. She seemed smaller to him, and he wondered if the whiskey he had drunk on an empty stomach was diminishing life for him. He drank to enlarge it. "I don't mean to be disrespectful. I can't help myself sometimes.

And don't worry. God has punished me plenty, believe me."

Jesus Maria did not respond and only looked at him closely. Leaving her sitting between two of her grandchildren, Miguel Chico went to his place farther from the aisle. He had promised his cousin Josie and her daughters Hanna and Rebecca that he would sit with them. They were a few seats away from his own mother and father.

"What did she say to you about the bondage and discipline?" Josie asked him immediately. "Really, cousin, you are too much."

Miguel Chico pretended not to hear what she asked and was looking over the heads of the congregation toward the altar. On one side, a chorus of children stood ready and expectant. On the other, crudely made statues of Mary and Joseph, a few shepherds, a donkey, a cow, and a pig were placed next to a crib filled with straw. For the moment, it was unoccupied and the plastic angel floating above the scene stared down at nothing. "I am a plastic angel," he said to Josie.

"Are you crazy? What are you saying?" She looked at him to make sure he had not drunk too much already.

Suddenly, the children began to sing "Silent Night" in Spanish and a very small boy and girl walked down the center aisle on their way to the manger. Above their heads, they carried a Woolworth doll wearing a diaper. Its eyes were a clear and deep blue and Miguel Chico saw them glide by sightless above the seated parishioners' heads. "Oh, my God," he said to Hanna. "It's the Chicano version of 'The Sound of Music.'" She giggled and watched a milky film of indifference form over his eyes.

"What did she say?" Josie asked him again and was disturbed by the tired look he gave her.

"You know, the usual," Miguel Chico said in a whisper, for the mass was beginning and they heard people shushing each other all around the gymnasium. "About how God is going to punish us." He winked at her.

"More?" Josie said, her voice full of sarcasm and humor. "I can hardly wait. I love bondage and discipline. It's more satisfying than confession."

"Mom," Rebecca said, smiling like her mother. "We are in church, you know."

"I was trying to forget it, dear, but I'll be good. Only for you will I keep my big mouth shut." Josie stopped smiling and looked toward the altar. Gabriel had begun the Nativity mass.

Uncomfortable in a chair that squeaked when she moved, Jesus Maria was thinking how much more she liked the "real" midnight mass at the Cathedral which was celebrated by the Bishop himself. She saw her son Rudy and Miguel Chico as the Bishop's trainbearers, still in their red cassocks and beautifully made white lace surplices, crawling about on their knees like adorable angelic snails. That mass was at midnight, not seven o'clock, and its liturgy had been mysterious and incomprehensible, as any-thing divine must be.

Jesus Maria opened her eyes and found herself in a worldly, unlikely hall listening to her nephew con-duct the sacred ritual in an unpolished Spanish and English that catered to the working classes and greatly displeased her. Gabriel asked them to stand and sing while holding hands. Again, she thanked God her mother was not with them.

Looking at Gabriel, she saw only her brother Miguel Grande's second son and not the representa-tive of Christ on earth. Jesus Maria blamed Pope John XXIII for permitting Holy Mother the Church to become a Protestant travesty. It was a wonder to her that he had not made it possible for priests to marry and to destroy Catholicism once and for all.

To keep from falling into complete despair, she turned her attention to the music. It was hardly Gregorian, and even though the children were sing-ing sweetly and with zeal, Jesus Maria could not rid herself of the feeling that they were all sitting and standing in some kindergarten class for grown-ups.

Again she shut her eyes and began going over the old prayers in her mind. Jesus Maria was especially fond of the *memorare,* a prayer she associated with the Little Flower more than with the Blessed Virgin. In the middle of saying it to herself for the third time, she was very startled when her granddaughter hugged her and said, "Peace be with you, Grand-mother," and even more surprised when she realized that she was expected to embrace those around her—including strangers—and wish them peace. She did it, but she did not like it.

At communion, all but her brother Miguel Grande, his son, and her niece Josie rose to stand in the main aisle. Jesus Maria saw that the three of them were giving each other knowing and scandalous looks for remaining seated, unrepentant, while the rest of the family was ready to receive the Lord in their hearts. She pitied them but felt they must fend for themselves in eternity. The way her brother described himself as a deathbed Catholic always got her goat, and the manner in which Josie and Miguel Chico ridiculed religion frightened and annoyed her.

She turned to see Josie's daughters in line behind her. At least their poor, lost mother had had the decency to bring them up in the Church. Josie might have lost her faith but not her reason. Slowly, Jesus Maria and the Angel family made their way toward the body and blood of Christ.

Miguel Chico sat, bored and tired, watching the procession of communicants and craving a drink. They reminded him of Dante's souls in Purgatory transformed into freeway drivers during the rush hour on an especially smoggy day in California. "But I'm in the desert," he said. Josie pinched him.

"Do you want me to go outside with you?" she asked.

"No, no, I'm fine. Just thinking out loud. Sorry." He wished the mass were still in Latin. He preferred it to the vernacular expressions of devotion his brother was valiantly attempting to teach his new parishioners. Latin at least sounded sacred to Miguel Chico's ears and in his altar boy years, he had learned it with enthusiasm. At dinner earlier that week, Gabriel had told them how only the younger generation was accepting the new mass with interest and some excitement.

The older generation, led by *la señora* Olguin, was against any change and campaigning hard for the restoration of one daily mass to be celebrated in Latin. Miguel Chico had no idea why Gabriel remained in the priesthood and bothered to serve such people. They struck him as superstitious, self-righteous fools.

"There's more to them than what you see," Gabriel said in their defense. "And that's what I want to get at."

"Well, don't expect them to know what you're talking about," Miguel Chico told him. "And don't expect them to thank you when you do find out what makes them tick. They'll hate you for it and run you off."

"You are such a cynic, brother. I believe in what the Church has to offer us."

Following the Bishop's orders, whether he wanted to or not, Gabriel was having to deny the elders' constant and irritating petitions. Early in the Christmas season, he had to inform *la señora* Olguin that she would no longer be in charge of training the children for their first communion and that as soon as the new year began, the young seminarians assigned to assist him would take on the task.

"But Father Gabriel," she said, a pink rosary flashing in her trembling hand, "I have been instructing the children for years." She had been instantly suspicious of this new priest sent to her parish by a bishop she distrusted.

"He's one of those Communist priests," she told Sonsa Trujillo in the first week of Gabriel's tenure. "He's more interested in politics than religion. You wait and see."

Gabriel had asked her and the advisory committee to help organize a campaign to feed the hungry of the parish. He even suggested that some of the less fortunate be allowed to attend committee meetings.

La señora Olguin believed in hierarchies and felt it her God-given right to decide who was to be admitted into the upper regions of the parish, where she held sway as head of its most important governing group. *La señora* had selected the members of her committee and knew they could be trusted to do what she told them. They included Sonsa Trujillo, Menso and Babieca Ortega, and the parish gossip, Sangrona Enriquez.

"I know, *Señora* Olguin," Father Gabriel was telling her. "But the Bishop, who asked me to extend his very best wishes and the appreciation of Holy Mother the Church, wants the seminarians to become involved with the children at an earlier stage of their instruction. I'm sure you understand." He used his most courteous Spanish when speaking to her and felt sorry for the old lady.

She replied politely and said that of course she understood and that she wished all of the young people in the parish nothing but success in their attempts to keep the children in a state of grace. Gabriel could tell by her tone that she included him at the top of the list of the young and inexperienced doomed to fail without her approval and guidance.

A few days later, *la señora* and a delegation of her cronies presented him with a petition demanding the reinstatement of the Latin mass, a petition they told Gabriel to deliver to the Bishop immediately. They made it clear that until he did so, they would not help him gain the confidence and trust of the many families in the parish, and that without the aid of her committee, Father Gabriel would be very isolated and unhappy. He thanked them and said he would do what he could.

"I would have told them to go to hell, especially since they believe in it," Miguel said when he heard the story.

"Be quiet, Mickie," Juanita said. "I think Gabriel handled the situation very well. Thank God Doña Marina is there to protect you from those people."

Doña Marina had witnessed the confrontation and after *la señora* left with her committee, she told Father Gabriel not to worry about them. "They're just a bunch of old people who care more about losing their power than about anybody's soul." He remained dejected.

"Persinada Olguin is just a hypocrite, Father. Don't let her get you down. Everybody knows she's been having an affair with the sheriff right under her husband's nose for years." Seeing that he was still troubled, she added, "If they become too much of a problem for you, I'll poison them." Gabriel smiled and excused himself from the table. Doña Marina was sorry he was bound by the privacy of the confessional and his belief in the goodness of others.

"I like that Doña Marina," Miguel Chico said. "Will she be at the midnight mass? I want to thank her."

"I doubt it. She won't have time. She's preparing the Christmas dinner for the Bishop. Anyway, she wouldn't know why you were thanking her."

The last of the communicants were returning to their chairs or walking out into the cold, clear night. Miguel Chico felt a draft at his back. He was looking at his brother with new eyes. Most of the time, he was indifferent to the Church and its rulings. He was unable to be indifferent about Gabriel, who filled him with pity.

Looking at Gabriel as he was giving them the final blessing, Miguel Chico saw him as a child under the chinaberry tree in their backyard scolding imaginary creatures in a language he had invented. No one in the family understood it. In the shade of the tree in bloom, Gabriel walked back and forth like a shaman in an old pair of Juanita's high-heeled shoes.

"Dopey, get back in the house. It's almost time for lunch," Miguel Chico called out to his brother from inside the screen door in the back porch. Juanita had taken them to see *Snow White* and Gabriel, clumsy and small for his age, instantly became one of the seven dwarfs to his cousins and older brother.

Standing on four-year-old toes, Gabriel told them, "Don't call me that. I am not that."

But they kept calling him that until the name became a term of endearment the Angels used when talking about Gabriel even after he had grown up. Juanita, who had not liked it at first, began to use it and Gabriel himself finally accepted it.

That moment of acceptance came on a Saturday afternoon in July. Gabriel had come into the house after his talks with phantoms and was on the bedroom floor struggling to free himself from Miguel Chico's stranglehold. Juanita, tired of hearing one or the other scream "Mother! he looked at me!" or "Mother! he breathed on me!" ran in from the kitchen bringing with her the smell of *caldo* and corn tortillas and two dinner knives, dull and rounded and harmless. She handed a knife to each of them and said, "There. Now. Kill each other." The three looked at one another and burst into tears.

At the table, the boys ate their Saturday lunch in silence except for the moment when, his face still burning with tears and shame, Miguel Chico handed

Gabriel a buttered tortilla. Gabriel examined it carefully and looked up into his brother's eyes. He set
the tortilla on the plate, salted it, and took a bite.
"You can call me whatever you want," he said, still
feeling the coldness of the knife in his hand. "I don't
care."

When they talked about it, the brothers laughed
about that afternoon and had not fought since, not
even about the Church. When Juanita remembered
the incident, she was embarrassed and asked them
not to remind her of it.

"How's Holy Mother the Church?" Miguel liked
to ask Gabriel in her presence.

"Just fine," she heard Gabriel reply. To her delight, he also said, "And grateful that you asked
about Her."

In a confident and strong voice, Gabriel had given
a sensible and happily brief sermon on charity. He
told them a modern day parable about a nun and
priest stranded in the desert, sitting and conversing
in the shadow of a dead camel. Most everyone
laughed and was enjoying the fun of the holiday.
Miguel Chico assumed that *la señora* Olguin and her
friends were not present.

"Has my brother finished?" he asked Rebecca.

"Yes, dear."

"Hallelujah! You know what I need."

In their teens, he and Josie had read *Wuthering
Heights* during the holidays so that they could be
depressed while Serena and the rest of the Angels

around them cavorted like happy, bouncing amoebae. In more recent times, Miguel Chico had begun drinking his way through the season and hardly remembered that December happened at all.

Following Josie and her girls out of the gymnasium, Miguel Chico remembered how Gabriel had looked at him at the end of the sermon, pointed to his wristwatch, and given him the okay sign for all to see. He had asked his brother to keep the sermon short and not too sweet.

"Well, half of this magic night is over," Josie said as they stood by the statue in the cold. "Are you going to Ricardo's with us, cousin?"

Ahead of them, walking slowly toward the cars, he saw Jesus Maria and his parents by the light of the Milky Way. "I'll go with you," Miguel Chico said.

V

A week before the Angels' fifth journey to midnight mass at Santa Lucia, Josie's mother prepared a family dinner. Eduviges served them her famous enchiladas and pan-fried quail. Hunting that autumn had been especially good to Sancho, and his wife had cleaned and prepared the birds for the freezer according to her own method for keeping them fresh.

"The quail is absolutely delicious, Tia!" Gaspar

told her. "Sensational!" Jesus Maria's oldest son was a gourmet and the first member of the family to earn a doctoral degree in the fifties. Over the years, his visits to Del Sapo had become more frequent and his mother never knew when he would appear at her door from his home in Chicago.

"I named him for one of the Magi and that's how he behaves," Jesus Maria said to those at her table. "Who knows what star he follows?"

"Don't start, Mother," Gaspar said. "You promised."

Juanita and Felix's widow, Angie, were helping Eduviges serve the dinner. It was Angie's first Christmas season without her husband.

The members of the older generation were seated in the dining room. Able to see and hear them, the other Angels were scattered among children and in-laws, who sat at card tables in the parlor and den. Even Jesus Maria's younger son, Rudy, was there. He had flown into town on business. He was a partner in a law firm in Washington, D.C.

"Long time no see, cousin," Josie said. "What brings you to visit us peons on the border?" Miguel Chico, Rebecca, and Hanna were at her table. "Girls, don't believe a word he says. Rudy's a lawyer."

"An immigration case is pending and I may get to work on it." He hugged her and looked at Miguel Chico with warmth. "Just checking on all you wetbacks, really."

They noticed he had gained weight and that he

still stood on his toes when he talked to them. "Welcome back to the perfectly happy family. Sit down and tell us about the big, bad world." Josie motioned for him to sit in the chair next to her.

Gabriel walked in. "Father Dopey!" Rudy stood up and hugged him. "Still keeping all the Mexicans in their place?"

"They're keeping me in mine," Gabriel said. "How are you, Rudy?" He greeted them all and told them he could not join them because one of his parishioners had died that afternoon and he had promised the mourners a special rosary. Jesus Maria was disappointed.

"Well, you can sit down and eat. They'll spare you long enough to do that," she said. "I need you here to support me against all the heathens in this house."

"No, really, Tia, I only stopped by to say hello. I'll see you on Christmas Eve." And he disappeared into the kitchen before his aunt could comment on the rude habits of the dead.

"Is my mother still trying to convert the whole world?" Rudy asked them.

"Of course," Josie said. "It's her mission and her cross, God love her."

"Jesus," Rudy said with humor. "I think the main reason we all went away to school was to learn how to explain that generation to itself."

"We know perfectly well who we are," his mother said from across the room. "It's you who don't know that we are all God's children, even if you don't believe."

"Mother, please," Gaspar said. "I want to enjoy my meal without any sermons."

"Here, Gaspar," Eduviges said. "I brought you another quail fresh from the pan."

"No one said we weren't God's children, Mom," Rudy replied, his deeply set dark eyes smoldering with pleasure. "It's just that we were wondering if God could be anything but a Catholic?"

"You are wicked," Josie told him.

"Can't help it. Except in this town, where else can we talk about God like He was some sweet Great-Uncle handing out Christmas candy canes to everybody?"

"Please, don't start her," Gaspar said to his brother. "I'll go home."

"Tell us about Washington," Hanna said.

"I thought you'd never ask," Rudy said, winking at Josie. "Actually, it's a lot like this town, you know. Only there, if all the black people quit working for one day, the whole world would notice it."

He put his arm around Rebecca, like a spy ready to divulge a secret. "Nobody seems to care much about us Mexicans there. But I bet that if every Mexican in this town stopped doing whatever they do for twenty-four hours, this All-American city would sure be hard up and hurting."

"What's Rudy saying?" Mema asked at the dining room table. She refused to wear a hearing aid.

"About how Mexicans should be like black people," Aunt Trini said. "Pass me the *salsa,* please."

"That's not what he said, Aunt Trini," Josie said quickly. She did not want to hear at the next family gathering that her cousin had turned into a Communist.

Breaking into the silence that followed, Juanita asked them if they had read about the death of Epifania Gutierrez. "The papers said she was ninety-seven years old. Can you believe it?"

"Impossible," Jesus Maria said. "She can't be that old. She used to take care of Gaspar. The newspapers always lie. I've stopped reading them."

"Why on earth would they want to lie about an old Mexican lady's age?" Gaspar was beside himself. He did not know if he wanted to howl with ridicule or anger.

"Because the Angels never want anyone to know how old they are," Josie said. "Ignore it and deny it is the family stance toward reality." Josie believed in reality. "You've been away too long, Gaspar."

Out of the void, Trini said, "I don't think we're like Washington, D.C., at all."

"No psychology course I ever took prepared me for this family," Miguel Chico said under his breath so only Hanna and Rebecca heard him.

"Age has nothing to do with anything," Jesus Maria said gloriously. "The soul has no age. It is eternal."

"I'm leaving," Gaspar said and rose halfway out of his chair.

"Sit down, Gaspar," Sancho told his nephew with a smile. "After dinner, I'll take you out to the garage. Your father, you, and I will smoke cigars and talk about sports and beautiful women. Relax." Manuel nodded with pleasure at Sancho and Gaspar.

"If this family weren't so crazy, we could talk about anything like grown-up people," Josie said.

"Look who's calling who what," Miguel Grande said. "Like it or not, Miss Brat, you're part of this family."

"Yes, I know. I was crazy to come back to it." Josie was still speaking with some humor, but Miguel Chico noticed that the small birthmark on the back of her neck was getting intensely red.

"May I have some more enchiladas, Serena?" he asked.

"Of course, darling. Be right back." She whispered into his ear, "Keep them from coming to blows and don't let anyone leave."

"We don't even have the same kind of weather here," Trini said, and sent Rudy into whoops of laughter. "I didn't know the nation's capital was in desert country."

"It's not, Trinidad," Mema said. "Please forget about it. I'm sorry I asked."

"We would have been better off in the fields," Rudy said and wiped his eyes. Only those at his table heard. He stood up and raised his glass of beer melodramatically. "The Angel family has finally made it into the middle class. Hated by the workers and taxed to death by the Great White Fathers!

Here's to Chicanos in the middle class!" He gulped down his drink.

"Now what's he saying?" Trini asked Mema.

"Nothing. Drink your highball, Trini."

"This is the greatest country in the history of the world," Miguel Grande said.

"I'll drink to that!" said Ricardo, who had been quietly eating his dinner.

"I sure hope my uncle meant that as a joke," Josie said and put down her glass.

"Well?" Rudy said. "Isn't anyone going to drink to the Chicanos?"

"Does anyone want more to eat?" Serena asked them. She was carrying a platter of steaming enchiladas on a bed of refried beans and melting cheese.

"I don't like that word," Jesus Maria said. "We are American citizens from Mexico. We are not what you are calling us, Rodolfo."

"And what is that, Mother? Say the word. It won't kill you."

"No, I won't," she said, helping herself to more beans. "You can't make me."

Rudy stood again. He pretended to be more tipsy than he was and spoke with a Mexican accent. He paused and put his right hand over his heart.

"The truth is," he began very quietly, "we don't know what we are because we don't know where we are. And where are we?" he asked in a louder tone. "Just like our souls are between heaven and earth, so are we in between two countries completely different from each other. We are Children of the Border." His speech was beginning to sound like a *corrido* played and sung by *mariachis*. All were mesmerized.

"And Uncle . . ." Rudy made a gesture directed at Miguel Grande. "You brought up history. I'm glad, because usually everybody wants to forget it or change it to suit themselves. This was Mexico before it was the land of liberty and equality for some. And before that, it was Indian territory. They knew how to live in it. So where are we?" he asked again dramatically and with a smile that charmed Hanna and Rebecca.

"We are on the border between a land that has forgotten us and another land that does not understand us." He raised his glass higher than before and held it with both hands like a chalice. Some of the children giggled.

"So what are we educated wetbacks and migrant souls to do?" He had been editor of the *Law Review* at Berkeley during the Free Speech Movement. The house was silent and waiting.

"Let's keep the border and give both lands back to the Indians!"

Rudy's toast was greeted with a roar of laughter and applause from some, nervous titters and sorrowful looks from others, and shrieks of delight from the children when he staged a pratfall and spilled beer on his creamy shirt. Before he sat down, Rudy made the sign of the cross over them.

"Hey, Rudy," Ricardo asked. "How much do they pay you for that Chicano rhetoric in Washington?"

"Not enough," Rudy said.

"I apologize for my ill-bred son," Jesus Maria said, quite taken by his performance.

Angie wiped tears from her eyes and said, "I wish Felix was here." Serena put her arms around her.

"Well, I'm glad Mama Chona is not," Trini said. "She wouldn't have stood for this one minute."

"Oh, be quiet, Aunt Trini," Josie said. To Rudy, she spoke under her breath. "Now you've done it. You'll get my mother into her Indian speech and I'll have to leave."

"I'm getting out of here," Gaspar said.

"Nobody is going anywhere," Eduviges said. She meant it. "I made *flan* and *sopaipillas* for dessert."

The children cheered.

vi

Jesus Maria and her husband, Manuel Chavez, were from the working class and had lived for fifty years in a small, red-brick house in the old part of town near the Cathedral. They had spent their marriage there in one long argument about money and the Church.

Manuel died in the spring of the same year that she hurt her arm, and Jesus Maria readily used the traditional mourning period and the more present ache in her right shoulder as excuses for not taking part in the annual Angel family holiday festivities. It was the eighth year they were to be held at Santa Lucia, and Jesus Maria was again amazed by the treachery of Time, her most vicious enemy.

"Eight years! It's not true. It's awful the way I cannot tell one year from another. I hope I don't become like Mama Chona in her last years. Yesterday, I opened the refrigerator door and could not remember what I was looking for, Mema. Don't tell anyone I told you. The family already thinks I am extinct, I don't want them to think I am demented."

Mema was taking in her older sister's pauses and the pitiable glances she gave her shoulder. The sisters were enjoying a late morning cup of chocolate while waiting for Serena to take them grocery shopping.

"I simply cannot make that trek across town anymore and especially in my present condition. And without Manuel. Well, it's impossible."

"Of course you can't, sister. It's your duty to stay home and be miserable by yourself." Mema did not bother to remind Jesus Maria that Manuel had consistently refused to attend midnight mass in any parish, no matter what year it was.

"I know you are making fun of me, but really, I still do not understand why they had to move the get-together out there. Honoring Gabriel in the first year was enough, don't you think? I am more than tired of everything changing around me. And for the worse. Only yesterday, I noticed some criminal has destroyed the Miguelito vine that's been growing on the fence next door for years."

"No?" Mema said, truly astonished.

"Yes. I can tell you that would not have happened if *la señora* Itturalde were alive. The beasts did not even have the decency to wait for a month after her funeral. It's horrible. I miss her so much."

It was the first time Jesus Maria had mentioned her best friend's demise and Mema was surprised. Ordinarily, her sister ignored death's visits to family and friends and changed the subject when she heard that someone she knew had been carried off into eternity.

"You'll just have to go without me," Jesus Maria said and wiped her eyes.

"Don't decide now. Wait and see how you feel that day." Mema was rinsing their cups in the sink.

"Why should it be any different from the way I have felt since Manuel took it into his head to leave me? I intend to feel terrible for the rest of my life."

Mema was relieved by her sister's exaggerations, for the truth was that after her husband's abrupt death, which she took very personally, Jesus Maria began to enjoy her solitude. Its silence was a daily, if not glowing, visitation she had not desired or expected, and she found herself in a state of fearful wonder gliding from one room to another like a nun in an empty convent. Only Mema's frequent visits kept Jesus Maria in touch with the outside world.

Manuel had not been a believer, at least not when in his wife's company, and had felt it his duty to champion the opposite side of any religious issue Jesus Maria raised throughout their marriage, whether or not he agreed with it. Over the years, they had grown deaf, though neither admitted to it, and their arguments louder. Sometimes, since they always guessed how the other was going to respond, they shouted in counterpoint, completely ignoring and disorienting Mema and Gabriel or anyone who might be sitting with them in Jesus Maria's living room.

Like many in her generation of Angels, Jesus Maria deeply believed she was a sinner, and daily mass in the desert was a penance she gladly imposed on herself. The few short prayers the priests at the Cathedral asked her to say at the end of her weekly confession were not enough for her and besides, she loved attending early morning mass in the most impressive church of the town. That she could see its steeple and bell tower from the swing on her front porch made her feel even more secure about the place reserved for her in the afterlife.

"See them, children?" she had said to her young nieces and nephews. "They are the guardians of the soul. Whenever you feel tempted by the Devil in my house, look at them and they will keep you from all harm."

In her heart, marriage and bearing children had

been the real punishments, as written in the Bible and interpreted for her by the celibate priests of the Cathedral. "I feel closer to our Lord on Good Friday than on Easter Sunday," she confessed to one of them through the weathered screen.

"That's as it should be, daughter," he responded and sent her into raptures. If she suffered enough on this earth, the afterlife would take care of itself.

But when Manuel died, Jesus Maria felt a slight, undeniable shift in her view of the life to come. The change began on the day she fell. And she had fallen, as her mother would have been the first to tell her, because she was not minding what she was doing.

During her recovery, Jesus Maria enjoyed telling relatives and friends that the dining room carpet had ambushed her and that she would have been all right if Manuel, in his misguided attempt to break her fall, had not rushed in from the kitchen behind her and, helpless creature that he was, fallen on top of her. They both heard the snap. "Manuel felt it more than I did, the big baby."

She was in the hospital for a week with a broken collarbone, which mended more quickly than the doctors had predicted. They were amazed by how quickly she recovered "for someone her age." The compliment offended her more than the humiliating examinations they put her through, for any Angel worthy of the name was immune to age and death.

What did not heal—he was dead within three months of her fall—was Manuel's sense that her injury had been his doing. He was inconsolable and wept like a child those days at home without her. With trembling shoulders, he sat in front of the television set and flicked the remote control from one channel to another until the colors ran together like the quilt on her bed. Dry-eyed, he visited Jesus Maria twice a day at Hotel Dieu, Del Sapo's Catholic hospital.

Toward the end of her stay in what she described as "that immodest place," she asked, "What's wrong with your eyes, Manuel? They're all puffy. Have you been drinking?"

"Nothing," he said in a normal tone of voice, and no, he had not been drinking. He did not look her in the eye and rushed out without saying good-bye when Gabriel walked into the ward with a bunch of winter chrysanthemums from Tovar's Flower Shop.

She was not sentimental enough to believe he had been weeping for her and dismissed the thought that Manuel was blaming himself for the accident. After her morning prayers, Jesus Maria finally decided that the puffiness around his eyes was a symptom of his need for new reading glasses.

"Men are such children, *comadre,*" she said to her sister-in-law Juanita. She had come to help Jesus Maria leave the hospital because Manuel was not able to take time off from work that day.

"What are you talking about, *comadre?*" Juanita asked.

"Manuel. He looks worse than I do and I'm the

one with the broken bone. I know that all he's eaten while I've been away are bologna sandwiches. I can smell them on his breath."

"Not every meal. Your brother and I have taken him out a couple of times," Juanita said. She loved both her in-laws and had seen from the start what an impossible pair they were. "But yes, I think you're right about men."

Shortly after her twenty-fifth wedding anniversary and in despair about her husband, Juanita asked her sister-in-law when she had felt the first real sense of disappointment in her marriage. "The day after my wedding," Jesus Maria had answered without blinking.

"Women are stronger. Can you imagine men bringing up children? They'd crack within the first hour, the poor weak creatures. Life is too hard for them, *comadre,* and they can't take care of themselves." Jesus Maria gave Juanita her nightgown to put in the small suitcase on the bed.

"Poor Manuel," she said with a great sigh. A nurse's aide was wheeling her toward the front desk to be released. "His work is killing him, *comadre.*"

For many nights after his death, Jesus Maria found herself by Manuel's side when he broke through the flimsy screen between this world and the next. Every morning, she returned intact to this side of the grave without him, but not before she had peeped into infinity where, she was surprised to find, there was no blinding white light, no angelic choruses of welcome, not even her mother, who could

always be depended upon to be where she was supposed to be. Jesus Maria saw only a vast, unbroken
grayness and what she imagined to be the smoky
color of existence before form and light came into
the world.

"Is that all there is to it? How awful, Manuel. I'm
going back." Her dreams fell around her like shrouds
in the hour before dawn when she awoke mumbling
into the unfamiliar silence of a house without husband or children. Reaching for the quilt and sitting
up to feel its warmth around her, Jesus Maria was
not only anxious, she was greatly disappointed.

"I know you think I'm silly but it's my duty to
Manuel that keeps me from going to Santa Lucia this
year, Mema." In the pause that followed, they heard
the noise of the bus pulling away from the corner
across the street.

"You know, Mema, there's not much to the afterlife."

"Oh?"

"I dream about being there with Manuel all the
time and then I feel awful about it for the rest of the
day."

"You have to die first before you can feel what
it's really like," Mema said lightly. She was surprised
when her sister remained quiet.

"Are you sick? Is your shoulder bothering you in
this cold weather? I saw frost over everything on my
walk over here this morning."

"I'm fine," Jesus Maria said after another long
silence. "Right now."

vii

During Christmas week of the eighth year, frost covered the mountains and the desert every day. It fell soon after sundown and transformed every parish of the town into a gleaming, treacherous terrain.

Jesus Maria watched it appear out of the bare, blue-black branches of the Vitex tree in the backyard, where it remained throughout the night and did not fade until long after her return from seven o'clock mass. "It's too cold to snow," she said to Mema on Christmas Eve morning.

"You're not going to Santa Lucia, then?" Mema asked, stirring honey into a cup of *manzanilla* tea.

"I am not about to fall and break another bone in my body. Is there any tea left?" She took off her coat with great care and laid it over the chair. "What time is it, anyway?"

"Eight o'clock. Here, take this. I'll make myself another cup." Mema put water in a small saucepan and sat down with her sister until it boiled.

Up the hill from them, on the fringes of Kern Place near Mesa Street, Miguel Chico was slowly waking up. He felt the dry desert cold in his nose, looked out of the window, saw only frost on the lawn and iron gratings, and went back to bed. From the kitchen, the voices of his mother and father broke like chimes into his reveries and the knot in his chest tightened. The morning demons were wrapping barbed wire around his heart.

"Jesus Maria just phoned," Juanita was telling Miguel Grande. "She's not going to be at the mass tonight."

"That woman is going to grieve herself into the grave," he said. "She's still alive. Why doesn't she act like it?"

Miguel Chico did not hear his mother's reply. He turned to lie on his left arm after adjusting the plastic appliance attached to his side a few inches below and to the right of the navel. He had lived with these bags for almost six years and minded them less than what the devils were doing to his head. They sneered and reminded him of the promise he made to Josie to attend mass at his brother's parish. Josie had not succeeded in persuading the family to congregate at her new house on the west side of the mountain afterward. Peeved, she decided to prepare a special Christmas Day lunch for a select few and to let everyone know about it. Miguel Chico agreed to be part of the revenge plot.

The demons at his heart were taunting him with his own words of the day before and conjuring up the face of their old family friend Herminia Terrazas, who had adored him. He had just flown in from New York City on his way back to California. Suffering from jet lag and once again disoriented by the desert light, he was shakily arranging his toilet articles in the bathroom when he overheard his mother tell Gabriel about Herminia's last days.

All her married life, this humble woman had devoted herself to a husband who demanded that his dinner be served at 5:30 exactly, not before or after, and berated her when one of their five children kept her from doing her duty. She was a woman who attended daily mass and served others with kindness and without complaint even after she herself became ill.

"I was with Herminia two days before she died," Juanita said to Gabriel. "The doctors had her on chemotherapy for over a year. For months, she couldn't keep anything in her stomach. And she was such a good cook. Remember how you and Mickie loved her oyster stew? She was so wasted away, I could hardly bear to look at her."

Miguel Chico saw himself pick up a drink from the shelf and stand just outside the door to his parents' bedroom. His mother was almost finished with the story.

"You know what she asked me, Gabriel?"

His brother said nothing.

"She asked me, 'Why did our Father make me suffer so much at the end?' Her beautiful eyes were full of pain."

Miguel Chico sailed into the room and heard himself say before Gabriel could respond to this sad tale, "Because 'our Father' is a sadist." Juanita told him to be quiet and to leave the room, that the story was meant only for those who knew that God worked in unfathomable ways.

"That's right," he had replied breezily, scotch in hand. "And people like you love Him for it. What a set-up." Herminia's face ascended, hovered, and disappeared through the ceiling. Miguel Chico got out of bed.

In the evening, he found himself looking over the set-up at Santa Lucia once again and watching his brother place one eucharist after another on the tongues of relatives and strangers alike. He had not taken communion for years and remembered only his panic as a child when the wafer had stuck to the roof of his mouth. In those days, they were not offered wine to help wash it down.

Hanna and Rebecca left the communion rail, walked down the side aisle, and returned to their places beside Miguel Chico. The coral necklace Josie had given Hanna for Christmas glowed against her navy blue velvet suit and cast a rosy sheen around her neck. She was lighter-skinned than her younger sister and had her father's small, round eyes.

Rebecca wore a red silk dress which made her blue-black hair shine and brought out the light cinnamon color of her skin. Her earrings, made of a mysterious substance Miguel Chico did not recognize, dangled and sparkled against the darkness of her hair.

Who are these gorgeous creatures? Miguel Chico

asked himself as they walked toward him. They were no longer children.

"Where did you come from?" he asked Hanna when she squeezed by him. When she did not answer, he asked Rebecca.

The young women ignored him, took his hands, raised them into the air, and gave thanks. Swallowing once more, Hanna said, "Don't worry. You didn't miss anything. Some of it is still stuck to the roof of my mouth, Uncle."

Rebecca smiled sideways at him and said, "God, that cheap wine tastes terrible." She stuck out a blue-stained tongue at him. "I sure hope Ricardo has some Bloody Mary mix at the party."

"You little lush," Miguel Chico said and gave her an affectionate pinch.

"Look who's talking," she said and pinched him back.

···
viii

Josie and Harold's marriage had lasted almost the entire decade of the sixties not far from the love-ins of northern California. Before Hanna was born, they drove from Cupertino to San Francisco to walk through the patchouli smells of the Haight Ashbury and to sit in Golden Gate Park and listen to The

Grateful Dead surrounded by lovey-dovey hippies in various states of ecstasy.

"My mother would think this the end of the world," Josie said to Harold the first time they found themselves among the half-naked, long-haired peyote devotees. When one of them asked her if she wanted a button, she thought her blouse was coming undone. Harold laughed at her and said that her mother did not have to worry about her daughter becoming a drug addict.

"Don't you sometimes want to try it?" Josie asked him, covering up her ignorance. "Just to see what all the smiling is about?"

"No," he said. "I don't like flying around inside my own head."

"Far out," said the hippie lying on the grass next to them at the Dead concert.

"Excuse me, sir," Harold said to him. "What's 'far out'? What I just said to my wife or the music?"

"Everything, man. Haven't you found it yet? It's all far out." His mercurochrome-colored eyes looked away from them.

"Leave him alone," Josie whispered to Harold.

When they argued, it was about Harold's military assignments, about how often they took him away from home, and about how much Josie wanted a stable life for Hanna and Rebecca. Two years before he walked out on them, Harold told her he was putting himself on reserve and intended to be at home more often. She was delighted and suspected nothing. The girls, five and seven, were in the same school where Josie was a part-time counselor.

Then one early afternoon in Spring, Harold kissed her good-bye, went to his job as projectionist of a local movie complex and, quite simply, never returned. He left to Josie the duty of explaining to the children that she did not know when their father would return or even where he had gone, which was the truth.

In the first week of his absence, she phoned the police and all the emergency rooms in the Bay Area. His boss told her that Harold had left at midnight as usual saying, "See you tomorrow." His commanding officer at the base had not seen or heard from him. She was in despair.

"Don't worry, Mrs. Newman," the officer said to her. "He's probably on a binge and will show up soon."

"Harold does not drink," Josie said. "It's been three days." She hung up.

"We'll just have to wait, girls," she said with as much conviction as she could muster. They looked at her with their cat eyes, kissed her good night, and went to their bedroom.

The moon was at the window and Hanna was hypnotizing it. "Look at the lady in the moon, Rebecca," she said. "She's combing her hair."

Like a small sleepwalker, Rebecca joined her sister. "Where's the man in the moon?"

"He's gone. Look at the lady," Hanna said. "She's nicer."

The silvery light turned the plants in the garden into enchanted dark blue shapes. A breeze from the ocean made them bounce and sway and filled the girls' nostrils with salt.

"They're ghosts," Rebecca said.

"No, they're not. Mom planted them. It's the moon that makes them look weird."

"They're ghosts," Rebecca said again.

To Miguel Chico, Josie's girls seemed possessed by the same spirit. He was writing his dissertation on Henry James in those years and warned Josie during his visits that if she were not careful, Hanna and Rebecca would drive her mad. He made such pronouncements with his hands crossed in an X against his chest and his head thrown back to look as much like King Tut as possible.

"You're the crazy one," Hanna said.

"All right, you two, you are hiding something. What ghosts have you seen since my last visit? Don't tell me any fibs. I want to know."

Hanna swore in her matter-of-fact way that she never saw ghosts and so did not talk to any.

"I don't believe you, Hanna. You're just scared to tell us because they made you promise not to, didn't they?"

"No, Uncle, really." They called him that out of affection even if, in fact, he was more of a cousin. "I don't believe in them."

Rebecca told him that her ghosts were made of ice cream and melted in her mouth. She licked her lips.

"You can't eat ghosts," Miguel Chico said. "They're made of air and light."

"Yes, I can," Rebecca told him seriously and asked for more real ice cream.

"What do they taste like, you little fibber?" Josie asked her. She found herself laughing as if Harold had not left them three months earlier.

"Like old marshmallow skins after you burn them," the child said, believing it. Josie looked at her carefully.

To her cousin, she said, "I do believe this kid is from another planet."

When she told them that after such a long time their father was probably not going to come back, Josie sensed how grown up they were. Hanna was the more sorry one because she had known Harold longer and had learned that fathers were supposed to be with their children. Rebecca, usually less shy than her sister, kept her feelings about him to herself and then one day asked Josie why she didn't have another baby.

"Because my husband is not here."

"Why don't you marry Uncle Miguel?"

"Because cousins do not marry. The baby wouldn't come out right."

"Why not?"

"Because it wouldn't. It has to do with the blood. I'll explain it all to you when you're older."

"Well, why don't you marry Aunt Serena?"

"Because girls do not marry girls. Girls marry

boys." She wished Serena were there to help her.

"Well," Rebecca said after a while. "When I grow up, I'll be a boy and marry you."

"Well," Josie said, trying not to laugh. "When you grow up, ask me and we'll talk about it then."

In the first year without their father, when they surprised Josie in a fit of weeping, the girls looked at each other like kittens in cahoots and silently agreed to take their mother's side, no matter what happened. They told her they would never leave her and made her cry all the more. "No, really," Hanna said. "We'll stay with you."

What else can they do? Josie asked herself in those early nights alone in bed. She did not dare feel sorry for them or herself. Instead, she woke from dreams of blind babies and turkeys mixed in with the faces of the people who had been at her wedding. At the end of one of those nightmares, Aunt Trini was flying around her with wings made of gigantic Chinese fans that suffocated Josie. In another dream, Doris Hansen visited her dressed like the Little Flower and chewing on roses made of chocolate.

She began spending the night in the girls' room in a sleeping bag on the floor. When her thrashing-about woke them, Hanna shook her out of the delirium.

"Mom, you're having another nightmare," she whispered. Rebecca was sound asleep.

"Yes, *mija*. Thank you. I'm sorry. It was Doris Hansen."

"Who?"

"Someone I knew in the desert."

"Is she here now?"

"No, no, *mija*. It was just a bad dream. Go back to bed. I'll go to my room."

"No. Stay where you are, please."

Other mornings before dawn when she could not sleep or dream, Josie went over her arguments with Harold. He had wanted to remain on active reserve and be available for intelligence work.

"You'll disappear forever or get killed in some awful revolution in Latin America," she had said.

"Probably closer to Viet Nam," he had replied. "Later, you can join me and see the world. I thought that's what you wanted."

"I did, but that was before Hanna." She was pregnant with Rebecca. "Now I want a home for them and no moving around until they're older."

"Whatever you want, Josie," he had said.

In the darkness, she chided herself for not seeing through his easy acquiescence. Guilt spiders crawled out of her mouth when she realized she had thought the children would keep him from leaving her. When she was angry in those dark hours, she sat itchily in the blue wool chair in her living room wearing a flimsy rayon nightdress and cursing men until she caught herself sounding for all the world just like her mother.

Finally, in one of her early morning rambles through the thorns, Josie stumbled upon a skin she thought she had shed cleanly and without regret or shame. The skin stuck to her ankles and reminded her that no woman could have an affair and not become entangled with the other man—the stranger, the friend, the lover, the not-husband.

It had been the secret of her life, known only to her and Serena. And him, of course. If Harold had suspected it, his intelligence training kept him from saying anything about it to her. Rubbing her back against the chair, it struck her—so complete had been her self-deception—that Harold had known.

He introduced her to Robert just before Hanna's first birthday. They were at a Fourth of July party at the Presidio.

"Honey," Harold said. "This is my old training camp buddy, Robert E. Lea."

"No, really? Like the general who caused the slaughter of thousands in defense of slavery?"

"No, ma'm," Robert said, affecting a southern accent. "It's 'Lea' with an 'a' as in 'pea.' It's my step-father's name." He spelled out both with a smile and was looking at her mouth.

"What does the 'E' stand for?" she asked. She was enchanted by the sound of his voice. From the celestial spheres, she heard Tia Cuca tell her that women fall in love with their ears and men fall in love with their eyes. Noses were also part of the formula, but she could not remember in what way.

"Earl, as in 'Duke of,' " he said, dropping the accent and taking her in with eyes so green that she faltered. For an instant, she was a child again and Uncle Armando was asking her to name the state capitals.

"Well," she said as naturally as she could. "So you're not from the South after all." She felt the pull of a wave as invisible as sound. "Well."

"Well, what?" he asked.

"Well, you've certainly slaughtered me. I've seen eyes that color only once in my life. They're beautiful, Mr. Lea with an 'a.' Where are you from?" Honest, small talk will save the day, she thought. Even with the windows and doors to the veranda wide open to the incoming fog, Josie was finding the room stifling.

"From Oklahoma," he said. "I grew up on a reservation there until my mother married my stepfather. I'm a Cherokee with some French thrown in."

"Oh, no!" Josie said, laughing. "It's too perfect. Just like in a novel."

"What's perfect?"

"Nothing," she said. "Your eyes."

Josie remembered that Harold, sitting to her right had heard her last words to Robert. "Yes, doesn't he?" he said. "We used to tease him about them in camp. They're much too beautiful to be a man's. I think he's a witch in male drag."

At that moment, she felt grateful for her husband's presence. Under the table, Robert nudged her foot the way a child urges another to come out and play.

Josie nudged back, returning the snake bite. Harold stood and was helping a blond woman find her purse. It was under her wrap and she fussed over his concern.

"Sweetheart," she said to Josie. "You've got a terrific hubby. Take care of him, you hear?" To Harold, she only said good night.

"Who was that?" Josie asked.

"Her name is Mollie something or other. She's from a well-known San Francisco family, and she was talking to me about all these groups starting up in the area where people take off their clothes and raise their consciousness." Harold broke into a smile.

"When I take off my clothes, that's not what I intend to raise," Robert said.

He is an Indian, Josie thought, and laughed at his comment. Mother, may I? She knew the answer.

"Harold, we need to go home. I want to feed Hanna before eleven o'clock. She's just getting used to the bottle."

She had spoken automatically, submerged in the sound of Robert's voice every time he responded or asked her a question. She wondered how someone can drown in another's voice and watched herself go under from a great distance.

"You're not staying for the fireworks? I hear they're stupendous if the fog stays on the other side of the bridge," Robert said. He was enjoying himself and Josie saw a way to rescue the drowning woman by dismissing him as a flirt. She thought that "stupendous" was one of the silliest words in the language.

"I would love to meet your daughter," Robert said. "Harold does nothing but brag about her. And about you," he added without a trace of irony. Josie believed him and decided to forgive him his voice and eyes and treat him like an ordinary human being.

"Come for dinner soon," she said.

"Yes, Robert, do that," Harold said. "I'll call you tomorrow and we can set up a time."

The men shook hands and patted each other's shoulders. Josie kept her hands to herself and smiled kindly at Robert. "Very pleased to meet you, Duke Lea." She hated to think she was flirting.

"The pleasure was all mine, Mizz Newman. Consider me your slave." He was a southern gentleman again and bowed.

She had laughed in the face of another wave heading toward her, larger and more powerful than the first, turned her back to it, and walked away as quickly as she could without seeming to be in a hurry. So this is what happens to girls brought up on Hollywood movies, she thought.

On the way out after getting her coat, she glanced toward the buffet table and saw a cadet slip and slide head first into the punch bowl. When she was waiting for Harold in the car, she could not think how she got there.

"What are you laughing about?" he asked.

"Didn't you see that poor guy fall into the punch bowl?" she asked, barely able to control herself.

"No," he said. "No, I didn't."

Josie laughed louder.

On their way home, the invisible fireworks exploding behind them like hundreds of comets, Josie began talking about the time she and Miguel Chico had gone to see Garbo in *Camille.* "I could have killed Mickie at the end when he started to laugh. I had never seen a sadder movie. I wanted to strangle him." Her voice went on by itself.

"Later, he told me he was laughing so that he wouldn't cry. I forgave him. But I don't think men know what women feel."

She could not believe her triteness. But she did not care what she said. She was talking to keep another sound at bay. "I don't know what men feel most of the time, Harold."

"Oh, Josie," he said. The lights from the oncoming cars flickered on and off his face. "You and Mickie have seen too many movies. If you want to know, I think most men go around feeling guilty. Either because they're not doing what their mothers expect of them or what their wives want them to do." His voice, ordinary and plain, brought her back to earth.

In a lighter tone, he said, "We boys are just confused little creatures whose daddies didn't show them the way." He reached for her hand.

"I think that's true," she said, meaning it. She

was quiet from Palo Alto to Cupertino. The sound of the ocean was in her ears and her hand was a piece of driftwood in his.

When she thought about Robert in those sleepless nights alone, it was as a comet that had passed through and collided within her, leaving only fading flashbacks of smooth skin and the smell of green grass in hair wet with lovemaking. She was blinded by his love and she went to him as often as she could with the unerring sense of the sightless tapping white canes along familiar paths.

"It's never enough, is it?" he said.

"Yes, it is," she answered. "That's why I want more." And in a small house on Levant Street in the Twin Peaks area of the City, he took her hunting and fishing in his lakes and mountains.

For two months, she was numb to all that was not him. As if hanging upside down from a tree in some prehistoric forest, she watched another woman pretend to care about her husband and child, her housecleaning, the laundry, her counseling, food on the table. With Robert, she was in a land where no bridges spanned rivers because no borders existed.

And as quickly as they had come together, they parted. Josie found herself back on familiar ground, looking up at an ordinary California sky, miraculously intact and pregnant. Ah, she said to herself with a tender smile, the brightness of the tail lingers on. She phoned Serena in the desert.

"Guess what?" she said.

"You're pregnant," Serena said immediately.

"Yes, dear. But there's more to it than that."

"I know. It's an immaculate conception. Mother will be so happy. At last, a virgin birth in the Angel family."

"It ain't no virgin birth, believe me." She told Serena she did not know who the father was. Without saying Robert's name, Josie said, "I mean, I know who he is, but I don't know which one is the father."

After a few moments of crackling along the long-distance wires, her sister asked, "What do you want me to do?"

"Oh, Serena, I only know I want the child. I don't care whose it is. I just know that it's mine."

The sisters agreed to tell no one, not even the child. When Rebecca was born, Harold and Josie asked Serena and Miguel Chico to be her godparents. Baptizing the child was the concession Josie made to her sister for sharing the great secret of her life. "What makes religious people think that a child is not born holy already?" she loved to ask, knowing that no one in the family would bother to attempt an answer. They believed in original sin.

Miguel Chico agreed to be part of the ritual but not before an argument with his cousin. "God, Josie, you are just like every smart Mexican Catholic sinner I know. You hate the Church and then you get married and baptize your children in it. Sheep. All sheep."

"I just don't want Mother and my sisters on my

back for the rest of that child's life. I bet if you had kids, you'd baptize them. So stop being such a priss."

"If I had kids, I'd lock them in their rooms to protect them from the world and ruin them that way. All right, I'll do it but I don't like it."

Miguel Chico felt his cousin's joy and swallowed his own feelings about the Church with scotch and soda. Later, Rebecca's wailing throughout the ceremony kept him from sneering openly as he sprinkled the child's head with what seemed ordinary water to him.

"I told you she wouldn't go for it," he said at the party afterward. "Remember when Rudy and I drank holy water before our first communion and got sick as dogs?"

Robert had been invited to the celebration but was not able to attend. His unit had been put on alert and was on its way to Viet Nam. He sent a silver spoon with Rebecca's name engraved on it. The note read, "I am very happy for the three of you. She will be a special and magical child. With love, Robert."

"That's nice. Conventional, but nice," Josie said and handed the note and gift to Harold. "I hope he doesn't get killed over there." There was nothing more for her to give him.

Harold said nothing and went about making their guests comfortable. The casual, faraway tone of Josie's voice when she talked about Robert rang in his ears. When he looked in on the girls, sound asleep in their parents' bedroom until the guests went home, Harold noticed for the first time how much Hanna resembled him.

Serena was half asleep on the bed with the children. Harold told her to go back to the party. "They'll be fine. The next feeding is an hour away."

Before she closed the door, Serena saw him smooth the blanket over Hanna and touch his lips to her forehead. "You're mine," she heard him say.

She walked down the hall toward the laughter in the living room. The sense that men and women were not strong enough to have children filled her with compassion.

Four years later when he left them, Harold did so without a word. Josie waited a year before she filed for divorce. She had decided to return to the desert with her daughters.

After the court hearing, which disappointed Josie and Miguel Chico with its dry and matter-of-fact brevity, they went back to the house in Cupertino. They emptied closets and cabinets, watched the furniture crated and shoved into a moving van, and vacuumed every room from floor to ceiling. Hanna and Rebecca helped by staying out of the movers' way and packing their own things.

Before supper, Miguel Chico told the girls a story about a Japanese prince. Josie could hear them from the kitchen.

"This story," her cousin said, "is about images made of words. You have to listen very carefully or you won't get it. Are you ready?"

"What's an image?" Rebecca asked, already bored.

"It's like a picture or sometimes like what you see when you look in the mirror. Now, be quiet and let me tell you the story."

"That's not fair," Rebecca said. "I can't see with my ears."

"What's wrong with you? Josie, this child has no imagination," he said loudly toward the kitchen.

Hanna poked Rebecca in the ribs and told her to be quiet. Josie was worried about her older daughter. She had been too quiet during their last week in California.

"Thank you, Hanna. If you really listen, the words will go into your ears and land somewhere inside your body. I want you to tell me where after. Okay?"

The girls were sitting on boxes filled with books across from Miguel Chico. They were unaware of Josie's presence as she looked at them from the dining room. She was struck by the distances between people and the feeling frightened her.

"Is it a long story?" she called out to Miguel. "Supper's almost ready."

Surprised, he looked at her with exasperation as she walked into the room. "No, cousin, it's not long." Her fear vanished when she sat down on the floor between the girls.

"Once there was a Japanese prince who had never seen a morning glory. He was told about a lord in a distant province who was a master at growing morning glories."

"How strange," Hanna said and Rebecca repeated her words in the same tone.

"Be quiet, girls, or we'll be here until midnight," their mother said. "Go on, Miguel."

"It was said that this lord had acres and acres of this flower in all colors of the rainbow."

"How pretty!" Rebecca said with a squeal. She was pretending to be interested.

"I'm warning you, Rebecca. Be still or I won't give you any hot dogs."

"The prince sent a messenger to the lord. He invited his highness to visit his estate on a certain day in the middle of summer.

"Riding through the lord's province, the prince saw only field after field of trampled vines and broken trelises as if terrible winds—like the kind that blow in Del Sapo—had torn everything that grew there into shreds. When he arrived at the lord's palace, no one was there to greet the prince and all the doors were open.

"The prince walked into the emptiness of the great hall. And there, on a table in the middle of the room, was a single, perfect morning glory floating in a simple peasant's bowl."

"I don't get it," Rebecca said after a few moments of silence. "Is it over? What happened?"

"Don't you see? It's not a story about what happens. There's nothing to get, silly. What do you feel when you hear about that one single flower floating in the bowl?"

"I feel hungry. Can we eat now?" Rebecca was looking at her sister.

Hanna was weeping. Her small shoulders were shaking and her face was in her hands.

"My God, Hanna. What's the matter?" Miguel Chico knelt before her and was trying to raise her head. "It's just a story about putting words to something that's very beautiful."

Josie signaled him to leave the child alone, but he could not bear her tears and tugged at her hands and chin. "Please, don't cry, Hanna."

She stood up and blew her nose. "It's not about that," she said and went on weeping.

Miguel Chico was beside himself and felt foolish on his knees. Josie put her arms around Hanna. "Tell me. Tell me what you feel."

"Empty," Hanna said. "I feel empty."

The next day, while the girls waited for her in the car, Josie paid the last of the bills and watered the gardenia bush she had planted in the first month of living in the house with Harold. It was in full bloom. She picked off a few dead leaves and blossoms, chose one perfect flower and left it floating in a paper cup by the kitchen sink. She could not bring herself to destroy the bush. She felt it would haunt her in a desert too dry to offer her gardenias.

"It's greasewood and sage for you, my dear, as punishment for your sins," she said to the blossom in the cup. Josie smelled its fragrance through the lingering fumes of the cleansing powder she had used to scrub the sink.

She left the house without locking the door and hoped that Harold would return and look for himself into that void. In the car, the girls were engaged in one of the endless games they created out of the air and which only they understood. "Are we really going now?" Rebecca asked her.

"Yes, Miss Impatient. We're really going now."

The girls sang, "Do you know the way to San Jose?" all the way to the freeway and kept singing it long after they were out of California and almost to Del Sapo. Josie threatened to divorce them, too, if they did not give her poor ears a rest. At least they sang in key, but could they please sing something else?

As the landscape changed from a wet green to a dry beige, Josie made them memorize all the names of the Angel family and explained in what ways they were related. She also gave them their first lesson in Mama Chona's rules of perfection.

"But no one can be perfect," Rebecca said. "Those rules aren't fair." Josie smiled at the echoes from her childhood.

"Are we going to have to follow them?" Hanna asked. She was the more practical daughter.

"No," Josie said. "But I want you to know about them because your grandmother Eduviges is going to expect you to follow them. With her, you will pretend. With me, you won't have to. If you tell me the truth, no matter what it is, I'll stand by you. If you don't, I won't know what to do. There are some things you're going to have to figure out for yourselves. Just remember that life—"

"We know," Hanna said, and then, as if reciting a lesson, "life is not fair and almost nothing makes sense. Be kind to others and tell the truth to those you love."

"Good for you, Hanna. Were you listening, Rebecca?" She was asleep.

When she parked in front of her mother's house, Josie took Hanna and Rebecca by the hand, guided them up the walk, and rang the front door bell. The heat of Del Sapo in the summer did not impress her as much as the brightness of the light. She could almost hear it.

Josie had allowed the girls to wear shorts instead of dresses and warned them that their grandmother would not approve. "If she says anything about it, just keep quiet and let me do the talking," she told them.

She rang again, knowing that in summers, her mother wanted visitors to enter through the side door, which she left unlocked. Josie reasoned that they were more than visitors. After a few moments, Eduviges appeared on the other side of the screen door. She was smaller than Josie remembered but her expression was the same. It was as fierce as a hummingbird guarding its nest.

"You came after all. Serena told me you would," Eduviges said. She was neither joyful nor sad to see them.

Josie almost lost her nerve and collapsed in tears before her. "Yes, Mother, and we are going to stay." Her voice was unsteady and her hands were wet and still holding fast to the girls. "I have a job and I want my girls to go to good schools."

Eduviges kept her eyes on Josie. "Without a father, those girls are going to grow up badly and find themselves on the street," she said matter-of-factly and in that dead-certain tone that made the rebellious Angels in Josie's generation crazy with rage.

Josie controlled herself. She knew she must not give way to self-pity or anger or she and the girls would be lost and not only to the street.

"We're staying at Serena's until I find a house. I've saved enough money for a down payment." Josie assumed her mother's tone and let the words speak for themselves without emotion or judgment. She wanted to show her mother that in her way she, too, had tasted bitterness and survived. She looked down at her girls standing bravely in the heat and reflected light of the front porch. "I want Hanna and Rebecca to know where they come from," Josie said with a steadier voice.

Eduviges looked at the children at last. She had not seen them since their father had left them. Their faces were moist and shining. She saw that Rebecca was dark and had large, disarming eyes. They peered through the screen and into the house as if not caring what they found. Hanna looked more like Harold. Her light skin was flawless. Eduviges smiled at her with affection.

"What a lovely forehead you have, Hanna," she said. To Rebecca she said nothing.

Josie felt the ancient demons emerging from their caves. They gave her the push she needed to strike the first blow. With the half-smile of an Angel—part teasing, part serious, so that no one ever knew which to believe—she asked, "Is my father here or have you killed him?"

"Oh, Josie, of course, he's here. Come in the house," Eduviges said and unlatched the door. "He's in the garage with Ricardo. They're looking over the engine of his new car. That Ricardo has made something of himself."

Josie ignored her mother. "Girls," she said, "go and tell your granddaddy that we're here to stay."

"Where's the garage, Grandmother?" Hanna asked.

"That way," Eduviges said. She motioned with her forehead toward the den. "Go through there."

The women watched Hanna and Rebecca walk out of the parlor. Before Eduviges began talking about them, Josie looked into her mother's eyes and asked, "Aren't my little Indians beautiful?"

ix

Throughout his life, Mema's son Ricardo, like his aunt Jesus Maria, considered himself more Spanish than Indian and obeyed the dictates of the Church. Together, when they had to, Ricardo and Jesus Maria looked across the river with disdain. Every time their aunt told them that modern Mexico was founded on a fraud, Ricardo nodded in agreement.

"And it remains a fraud to this day. There was no Revolution. There was only an excuse for dolts and murderers to wallow in their errors and commit their crimes against innocent people. I do not begin to understand how decent people can live there. It fills me with rage and disgust every time I think about it."

Manuel and Ricardo knew that the phrase "decent people" meant middle-class Catholics. Mexico was on her mind because Jesus Maria had just returned from an afternoon visit in Juarez with yet another relative who had remained south of the border and was desperate for money.

"God, what a country," she said to them. "Salubria Lozano is at her wit's end trying to make ends meet. I gave her what I could for the children's sake but I know it won't solve her problems. What that country needs is a real revolution organized by someone who knows what he's doing and why he's doing it."

"Why don't you organize it, Jesus Maria, since you seem to know so much about it?" Manuel asked her. A World War I veteran, he had learned to mistrust all nations.

"Be serious, Manuel. Ricardo, tell him to be serious."

Ricardo's dream was to be a respected member of the middle class on the north side of the river. He was determined to see his children enjoy lives free from the prejudice against Mexican Americans who rose too high above their place in the second largest state of the Union. Happily, they did not have to suffer from the doubts about their place within the Angel family. Unlike him, they had been born legitimate and in the United States. That Mama Chona had loved and brought him up was in his favor. That she had adopted him and given the family name to someone with no name was an issue that had caused dissension in the family.

"No, Miguel, I will not call him brother. He is Mema's son. To speak of him as my brother is to deny the existence of his own mother. It is a scandal." Over the years, Jesus Maria had stuck to her views about Ricardo's place within the family, even after Mama Chona's death and her own increasing admiration for Ricardo's accomplishments. "Mema may have made a mistake, but she is and always will be his mother. Don't you forget that."

"Well, I think of him as the kid brother I always

wanted," Miguel Grande told her. "And that's what I'm going to call him."

"And what about your sister? What are you going to call her?" Jesus Maria was livid.

Miguel Grande looked at her in silence. After a few moments, he said, "Mema is my sister and Ricardo will be my brother. Do you understand?"

"I understand that his mother is being completely ignored. And she is the Angel in this mess."

"Well, Ricardo will now be an Angel legally," Miguel Grande said and walked out of her house.

"He is my nephew!" she shouted through the door.

Her nephew worked his way through the local college. Ricardo was not as brilliant as some of his cousins, but Jesus Maria saw that he was a less troubled and complicated person than her son Gaspar. In her mind, simplicity was closer to sanctity and she secretly admired Ricardo.

Like Gaspar before him, he joined the navy and was sent to Korea for one year. From Tokyo, Ricardo mailed navy blue pea-coats with Japanese dragons gorgeously embroidered in the linings to Rudy and Miguel Chico.

When he returned to Del Sapo, Ricardo was hired to do a government job that was not affected by the changes in the administration. His employers held him up as an example of what those from Ricardo's background could accomplish if they set their minds to it.

In his late twenties, he married a woman of great

kindness and humor from a German Mexican family. Josie was the youngest bridesmaid at their wedding. Later, the family heard that Alicia had been up before dawn sewing on the last of the tiny simulated pearl buttons and eyelets of the dress she had made for herself. She startled her mother by appearing at the breakfast table in all her bridal finery several hours before she was to walk down the aisle toward Ricardo.

"You must be anxious to leave your father's house," her mother said.

"No, Mamá. I am anxious to have a home of my own and I love Ricardo very much."

"I hope so, dear," *la señora* Haussman said, took off her reading glasses and admired her daughter from across the room. "That helps, even if it does not matter so much later on after the children come. Respect matters." Alicia's mother belonged to Mama Chona's generation.

Ricardo brought up his children to ignore their Mexican heritage and to live according to the myths of North America. He was confident that economic, if not social, success awaited them.

"With your last name," he said to Alicia, "they could have it all. As Angels, I'm not so sure, though they have more of a chance than I did. We'll see."

After he bought his home in Santa Lucia parish, Ricardo began asking others to call him Richard. Some of his buddies at the YMCA started calling him Dick.

X

"Well, shall we get on over to Dick's?" Miguel Chico asked Josie and the girls.

"Your mother said for us to wait for them by the statue to see who was driving with whom," Josie said. Her breathing sent white plumes toward him. When the breeze shifted, they floated over her shoulder toward the statue.

Juanita and Miguel Grande walked out of the gymnasium. "Are you going to Alicia's with us?" his mother asked him.

"No, Mom, I'll drive with Josie and the girls. I thought we talked about it already." The statue swayed and Miguel Chico moved to catch the eyeballs rolling out of its palm onto the frosty walk.

"What's the matter with you? What are you doing?"

The statue was immobile and intact, its offering still in hand and staring up at him. "Nothing. I thought I saw something move. Probably one of the kids. I haven't seen so many kids in one place in ages."

Juanita looked at him carefully. "You'd better show up at the party. I told Alicia and Ricardo you were all going to be there. She'll be very disappointed if you end up somewhere else."

"We'll be there, Tia, don't worry," Josie said and slipped her arm around her cousin. "Alicia told me that Doña Marina sent over some of her sweet tamales and I don't intend to miss tasting them. Come on, cousin. Girls, go ahead of us and unlock the car."

On the way, they stopped at the Mex-Tex Bar on Alameda Street. "It's our duty to be late," Miguel Chico said. "The Angels expect us to be rude and we mustn't let them down. It's all part of the ceremony."

Hanna and Rebecca were in the front seat and singing a popular song Miguel Chico did not recognize. Their voices were lovelier than the lyric. "I used to know all the songs in my day. Your mother hated me for winning all the talent contests at the birthday parties. Remember, Josie?"

"We know," Hanna said from the driver's seat. "You had the voice of an angel. Grandmother Eduviges tells us all the time about when you guys were kids." The young women began singing a Chicano version of "Jingle Bells." Josie and Miguel Chico steamed up the windows of the car with their laughter.

Hanna drove into the lot in front of the Mex-Tex Bar. "Is this where you want to go?" she asked.

"Now, now," Miguel Chico told her. "So it's turned into a strip joint. We'll regain our purity after mass by taking in the first show of the night. I won't have any middle-class Angel prudery in this group."

He opened the car door for them with a flourish and bow. "It's nice you children are almost old enough to drink at one of Del Sapo's finest establishments. Let me do the ordering."

The hot pink and chartreuse neon lights of the bar were very bright in the frost and hurt Hanna's eyes. Inside the door, not even Josie's cold kept her from smelling the beer and stale cigarette odors rising from the carpet. The waitresses, in short red velvet dresses and wearing Santa Claus caps that jingled below their waists, were spraying instant Christmas tree fragrance into the middle of the room. "That smell is worse than the bar's," Miguel Chico said. They were told that the first show was an hour away.

"Good. We'll have time for one round of drinks. Maybe two, if we're lucky. Ladies, I will join you soon. I must change bag number 14,792."

"You are so vulgar, cousin," Josie said. "And insupportable. Hurry up."

He bumped into a waitress rushing in the front door. "Sorry," she said and shook snowflakes from her coat.

"Is it really snowing?" Miguel Chico asked her.

"Yes. Not too bad. It won't stick. The ice on the streets is a killer, man, and it's cold as a bitch's tit." She laughed and pulled at his earlobe. "Smile, honey. It's Christmas." She had short, reddish hair and talked like a *chola* from the southside *barrio.*

"You're cute. Are you from here?"

"No. I'm visiting from California."

"What a waste," she said, standing back and giving him the once-over. "The little boys' room is down the hall to the right."

He changed his bag and began washing his hands. They were miles below him in a sink that had shrunk to the size of a *peso*. In the mirror, his reflection was obliterated by hundreds of snowflakes falling symmetrically into a void.

"Like big white Cheshire cats," his voice said. He shut his eyes.

Once, against all laws of nature, snow had fallen in the Bay Area. Miguel Chico and Sam Godwin walked through the streets of the university town in the early morning before any traffic sullied the whiteness of the world. The palms and oaks had offered them armfuls of snow.

"Like big white Cheshire cats," Sam had said in a cultivated Oxford accent. A native of Tularosa, New Mexico, just north of Del Sapo, he had been a Rhodes scholar and was in his Anglophile period. Miguel Chico, who was in his literal period, had seen only snow on branches.

They had shared a flat on Guerrero Street in San Francisco for three years. When Sam left California to be a corporate accountant in New York City, Miguel Chico felt the world had ended.

Six months later, hanging on to a shrunken sink in Del Sapo, Texas, he was still in mourning as only an Angel could mourn. Passion had led him to believe that the Sam he loved was real.

"Lead your own life," Sam's letters told him. "Please don't try to change mine. What you do have to change is the bag around your heart."

The sink returned to a normal size and Miguel Chico felt its coldness. Before him, the mirror cleared and returned his quick glance. He dried his hands and went back to the women waiting for him.

They were seated at a rounded booth in a corner of the almost deserted club. Plastic holly wreaths hung above the tables along the walls and featured tiny plastic cowboys and cowgirls eating chili dogs and drinking Coors beer. Electric *luminarios* lined the stage and flickered in red and green on the dance floor.

"You sure take us to the neatest joints," Rebecca said. She meant it. "I don't think Mom would let us babies walk into a hellhole like this by ourselves."

"That's right, baby," Josie said. "But we're with a gentleman, so it's okay. Even your grandmother would approve but only because Mr. Perfect brought us."

"They don't think he's so perfect anymore," Hanna said.

"I haven't any idea what you're talking about, *chavala mocosa,*" Miguel Chico said to Hanna. She knew he did.

"You have to stop writing about our perfectly happy family," Josie said. "The older generation does not approve. They think you're telling their terrible secrets to the world and they don't like it.

And don't call my daughter a snot-nosed brat."

"Some of the younger generation don't like it either," Rebecca said. "Grandmother told us that Ricardo read the whole book out loud to Alicia and that they both found it very upsetting, especially him." She sipped a pink and green margarita and gave him a beatific smile.

"Well, we knew Ricardo wouldn't like it," Josie said. "It's just envy. I keep telling them all it's fiction and they keep wanting to believe every word. They should be glad I didn't write that book. I'm not as nice as you are, cousin. I would have told the truth."

Miguel Chico's novel had been written during a sabbatical leave when he decided to make fiction instead of criticize it. A modest, semi-autobiographical work, it was published by a small California press that quickly went out of business. *Tlaloc* was an academic, if not commercial, success and its author became known as an ethnic writer. After seeing what the world did to books, he returned humbly to the classroom and to criticism.

"Maybe I ought to start telling the truth," Miguel Chico said. "Then they would really get mad at me, maybe even get a court order to keep me from coming back to Del Sapo. Sales would go up if I got murdered and cut up by some demented religious fanatic." The cowboys and the cowgirls in the wreath started throwing chili dogs and beer at each other. "I have decided," he said and stopped.

"What? What have you decided?" Josie asked. She was embarrassed for him. Rebecca and Hanna put on their disinterested cat expression.

"What?" Miguel Chico asked. The wreath was perfectly still before him. "Oh. I have decided simply to love them. At least their reaction is honest. The dumb sociologists want only positive images, whatever they are, from fiction writers. As if the whole world, especially their own little one, were one big happy collection of ethnic groups. No one knows how to read anymore."

His voice was getting louder and the waitress approached their table and asked if they wanted another round. "I was just telling my mistresses that I have made a Buddhist resolution to love my family, no matter what." He drank the rest of the margarita in one gulp. "It's much easier when I drink."

"Do Buddhists drink?" Hanna asked.

"I'll have one with you, Uncle," Rebecca said.

"This one does," he replied to Hanna in a serious tone. Then in falsetto he said to the waitress, "Yes, Mrs. Santa Claus, we will have another round. And bring us some *pico de gallo* and tortilla chips."

"No more for me, cousin," Josie said and raised her eyebrows at the girls. "You know we're going to stuff ourselves at Alicia's. I want to leave room for those sweet tamales. They are divine." She motioned the waitress away with a wave of her hand.

"Okay, okay. I'll do what I'm told and follow you

to the ends of the cosmos." Even he was getting tired of his performance.

Josie stood and put her arms through the sleeves of the purple wool coat her daughters had given her for Christmas. "Come on, let's go, children. I've had enough local color for the night. I am becoming a neon light and those wreaths are too scary for words."

Josie drove the rest of the way to Ricardo's. The frost was heavy and covered the streets and sidewalks with its treacherous sheen. She had trouble parallel parking across the street from Alicia's house.

The lights from the living room windows transformed the icy grass of the immaculate lawn into a golden magic trampoline. They saw the long shadows of the children inside bouncing upside down on it. Miguel Chico's heart moved with the shadows as he and Josie followed her daughters carefully up the walk.

"Are you all right, Mickie?" Josie asked him softly. "Girls. Get in there and slay them," she said with a laugh and nodded toward the windows. Hanna and Rebecca were ringing the doorbell.

Josie squeezed Miguel Chico's arm. Gently she said, "Behave yourself, cousin, or I'll have to take you home and punish you. Perhaps a little bondage and discipline?"

xi

His handsome profile outlined by the light from within and curly black hair gleaming with Vitalis, Ricardo greeted them warmly. He rushed them in out of the cold and helped them take off their coats.

"Hanna, Rebecca, how are you? You two get better-looking every year." They embraced him.

"Hey, Josie, Merry Christmas. You, too, Mickie. When did you get in?" He gave them his best smile and led them into the living room. "The latecomers have arrived," he announced. "Now we can eat."

No longer shadows on a wintry lawn, the children were served first. They sat around the Christmas tree on a newly purchased and stain-resistant carpet. Struck by their innocence, Miguel Chico felt sick with pity for them. Struggling against the feeling, he looked at the ornaments Alicia had made and saw painted straw figures holding tiny multicolored lights that turned the tree into a rainbow that stood still.

"Where's my brother?" he asked Ricardo.

"Which one? Gabriel or Rafael?" He knew who Miguel Chico meant. Rafael rarely attended any family gathering. After a silent moment, Ricardo said, "I think he's in the den. Let me hang up your coat."

To get to the den, Miguel Chico had to make his way through the kitchen where Alicia was arranging slices of turkey, smoked and spiced, onto a wooden platter she had carved and lacquered. She smiled at him with genuine affection.

"Hi, dear," she said. "Why haven't you come to visit us sooner? I'll hug you in a minute. My hands are too greasy. I'm so happy you came. Each year, it seems like there are fewer people or maybe my eyes are getting so bad, I can't see everyone." She laughed. "I miss Jesus Maria. I know she didn't come tonight."

"I miss her, too," Miguel Chico said politely. The smell of strawberries brought him out of a trance. The fragrance was vagrant and took him by surprise.

"Am I smelling strawberries in December?"

"It's my potpourri. I put it together myself. Do you like it? I'll give you some to take with you."

"It's wonderful." He felt himself beginning to pretend to enjoy the world.

Alicia dried her hands, took a handful of the crushed leaves and flowers, and held them to his face. "Isn't it great?"

They embraced and he felt her affection from a distance as he slid into a familiar stupor he blamed on everything but alcohol. "Can I have a drink?" he asked.

Alicia looked up at him. She could not keep her eyes from blinking rapidly and oddly in the light. Miguel Chico was afraid for her.

"Of course," she said naturally and shifted her gaze downward. "I don't think there's enough food."

"You say that every year, Alicia. I'm sure there's more than enough."

"I know. It just seems that way to me. The scotch is in the den. Have all you want." She carried the platter into the dining room where the grown-ups hovered like wasps around the table and helped themselves to her offerings.

"Have you tasted Doña Marina's tamales?" Miguel Chico heard Josie ask Alicia. He could see the women from where he stood, paralyzed, in the kitchen.

"Yes," Alicia said. "They're heaven, as ever. I could eat a dozen all by myself."

He saw Josie take a bite, taste the raisin, pine-nut, and quince flavors, and roll her eyes toward the ceiling. After a while, he was able to walk into the den. Gabriel was at the far end of the room. As if in a trench filled with blood, Miguel Chico went toward his brother.

"I need to talk to you," he said to Gabriel.

"Go to one of the bedrooms where we can be alone. I'll find you. Go on. You'll be all right." Gabriel touched him on the shoulder. "Go on," he said again.

Feeling Gabriel's touch like a burn on his arm, Miguel Chico bumped into Ricardo in the long hallway. He did not stop.

"Excuse me," Ricardo said and laughed for no

reason at all. In the den, he showed Gabriel how to get the record going and the music started up in all the speakers throughout the house. It was a popular *salsa* rendition of "I Wanna Wish You a Merry Christmas." Gabriel went to look for Mickie.

Watching him, Ricardo waited a few moments. Slowly, looking into each room along the way, he followed his cousin to the master bedroom at the end of the corridor.

Ricardo saw that the big eaters in the dining room were on their third helping and that his wife was still bringing food to the table, mostly sweets. Home-made fudge with pecans from their tree, the crumbly sugar-cinnamon cookies he loved, chewy cashew pralines, and three different kinds of sweet bread joined the last of Doña Marina's tamales. He knew Alicia had saved some for him in the freezer.

In the living room, Juanita and his cousin Julia were arranging the children into a conga line, begin-ning with the smallest. The few remaining members of the older generation, who refused to dance, sat on the sofas along the walls, clicked their tongues, and nodded their heads in sleep and conversation.

"Is Jesus Maria really all right?" Aunt Trini asked his mother.

"Yes, of course she is," Mema told her. "You know how strict she is about mourning periods."

"Hasn't it been a year?"

"No, Trini. He died last March, remember?"

"Are you sure?"

His mother turned away from her and asked Alicia if she could help her gather the dishes. "I'm tired of sitting and I can't dance. I might as well make myself useful."

Ricardo saw his children in the line with Josie's girls and his face flushed with joy. Serena came up to him.

"Wanna dance, cousin?" She had seen Miguel Chico and Gabriel disappear into the recesses of Alicia's house.

"No, thanks, Serena. I've got to check on something."

"Don't do it just now," she said, grabbing him with both arms around the waist. "Come on, dance with me. I need a man to dance me around the room."

Ricardo looked at her and laughed. Serena always brought her mother to the family celebrations and left her roommate at home.

"I'll do it after I use the little boys' room." She clung to him and after a turn and a half, let him go. The children laughed when she joined the conga line at the wrong end. Ricardo walked into the master bedroom.

"Let him go in love," he heard Gabriel say to his older brother. Miguel Chico was sitting on the bed with his back to the door, shoulders shaking, head bent in an ugly way, like a hanged man's.

"Come on, you guys," Ricardo said. "The fun's just starting. Everyone is asking where you are."

Miguel Chico straightened his head and did not turn around. Gabriel gave Ricardo a hard look.

"We'll be right there," he said firmly. "Is there any food left? I'm starving."

"Plenty, you know that." Ricardo walked away, leaving the door wide open.

"Oh, God," Miguel Chico said. "I hope he didn't hear anything I said. He's the last person I want to know about my life."

Gabriel took his hand. "He heard nothing. Even if he did, you know he wouldn't talk to you about it. Can you eat something?"

"No, you go ahead. Leave me here for a while. Close the door, Gabriel, and please don't tell anyone where I am." Miguel Chico blew his nose.

"All right, but if you don't join us in five minutes, I'm coming to get you. Remember what I told you."

After his brother closed the door, Miguel Chico surrendered to the devils. In matter-of-fact, reasonable voices, they told him he was not a child of the Church or worthy of the family name and that Ricardo should have been his father's firstborn son. Because what they said was true, the demons added, he ought to consider destroying himself.

xii

Across town and closer to the mountain, the frost fell more lightly. Unprotected, the swing on Jesus Maria's front porch changed from green to white.

Just looking at it when she turned on the outside light made her grateful to be alone and inside the warmth of her own home.

"I should have covered it or had it taken out to the garage," she said. "I told Manuel that paint would peel."

She walked into the kitchen, unchanged from the time she had married, put the kettle on the gas burner, and spooned some instant coffee into the mug Manuel had used for thirty years. He had preferred his coffee brewed and every morning before she went to mass, she had left it on the stove for him.

Jesus Maria saw Manuel and Gabriel waiting for her to serve them the *huevos rancheros* she had made for them.

"Your daughter Julia phoned while you were in church," Manuel said to her.

"What?" Jesus Maria asked. Lately, the cotton in her ears had grown thicker and harder to ignore. She found consolation in reminding herself that Beethoven had been completely deaf when he wrote the Ninth Symphony. When she was not putting herself through exercises of self-reproach, Jesus Maria enjoyed seeing her life reflected in the great figures of history and culture.

Manuel repeated what he had said.

"What did she want?" Jesus Maria responded as loudly as her husband.

"Nothing," Manuel yelled.

"Then why did you tell me?" Jesus Maria screamed in that half-serious, half-mocking angry

tone Gabriel and the family associated with her unhappy life.

"Please stop shouting," Gabriel said. He was trying hard not to choke on the laughter and eggs in his
throat.

"We are not shouting," Jesus Maria said. "We are
merely emphasizing our points." She paused and
looked at her husband. "Isn't that right, Manuel?"
she yelled.

She saw that the water was boiling. Manuel and
Gabriel vanished and once again, she was alone.

Gaspar had told her the story about Beethoven
conducting the Ninth Symphony for the first time.
She loved the moment when the concertmaster had
to turn the composer toward the audience so that he
could see, if not hear, the ovation they were giving
him. Like some of the lines in Sor Juana's poems, that
moment sent shivers up Jesus Maria's spine.

Stirring sugar into the coffee, she heard Gaspar
teaching his younger brothers and cousins the
themes of major symphonies in catchy phrases they
could sing in their soprano voices. "Poor Mozart's in
the closet, let him out! let him out! let him out!" Josie,
Julia, and Serena sang. And to the opening phrase of
Beethoven's Fifth, Rudy and Miguel Chico sang,
"Chile con pan!" in melodramatic tones and ran each
other through with imaginary swords.

Jesus Maria heard them still and wondered what
happened to children after their twelfth birthday.
"It's sex that ruins them," she said to Mema the day

she caught Rudy, Josie, and Miguel Chico under the house. They weren't actually doing anything, but their sullenness after she punished them for disobeying her orders and the way they looked at one another told her they had crossed the line into a land where she could not follow.

In the last years of Manuel's life, hardly any of their children came to visit and when they did, she sent them packing into nearby motels. When Juanita asked her at Eduviges' dinner party if any of them were coming for the holiday, "Of course not, *comadre*. They're too busy making money. Even Rudy is going to leave before the day itself, he hasn't told me when." They stopped being busy for a few days and attended their father's funeral.

Jesus Maria switched on the back porch light and walked into the room where Manuel had slept alone for over twenty years. She sat at the foot of the bed and felt the warmth of the mug in her hands.

Thank God Gaspar and Gabriel had been with her the morning she returned from mass and found Manuel on the floor by his bed. He had been putting on those awful argyle socks Jesus Maria hated so much and had wanted to burn every time she washed them. She imagined that his breath had caught halfway into his throat and that an invisible grenade exploded at the back of his head.

Manuel lay on his side, one sock on, the other in his hands, mouth and eyes open, body bending toward the toes of his right foot. While Gabriel and

Gaspar made phone calls, Jesus Maria struggled to remove the sock from Manuel's foot and wrenched her injured shoulder.

"God, Manuel, you've made me hurt myself again," she said, fully expecting him to respond. When he did not, she sat on the bed and was looking down at her husband and wiping her face with the detestable sock when Gabriel returned to the room.

"I did not expect this," she said to him furiously.

"I know, Tia. We never do." Gabriel spoke to her in as comforting a voice as possible. They both knew that Manuel was in his early eighties and had been hoping, like Caesar, to die an unexpected death.

Miguel Grande, Juanita, and Mema arrived. The men lifted Manuel onto the bed. Mema closed his eyes and then his mouth by tying a handkerchief under his chin and around his face as if he had a toothache. On their knees and resting their elbows on the bed, the mourners said the rosary from beginning to end. Gaspar excused himself before they began their prayers and, to his mother's great exasperation, disappeared for the rest of the day. Like some crazy woman, Jesus Maria heard herself babbling the words of the familiar prayers.

In shock and amazement, she went through the motions of burying her husband and accepting the condolences of friends and relatives with growing numbness. Her eyes teared from the allergies of a lifetime in the desert and not because she was weeping for her loss. In her mind, Manuel had not left her. She sensed his presence beside her even if others did not.

He was given a military funeral with full honors, and Jesus Maria, embarrassed by so much pomp and so many strangers in uniform, grounded herself at the graveside by staring at Gabriel as he recited the office for burial and sprinkled Manuel's coffin with holy water. Someone handed her a flag folded into a triangle.

She thought about walking into her house from the cemetery and busying herself by making certain that everyone had enough to eat and drink. From her childhood, she remembered the weeping Indian women dancing at the wakes for their dead so that the gods would see they were happy. After a few hours, she asked the remaining relatives to leave her alone so that she could rest.

"Are you sure you don't want me to stay the night with you, Mamá?" Julia asked her.

"No, no. Please, I'll be fine. And take Gaspar. I need to be alone in the house so that I can sleep."

When the mourners left her that early evening in March, Jesus Maria had locked the front door and faced the silence of her new life. Still sitting at the foot of Manuel's bed, Jesus Maria saw that old self walk from room to room, flag in hand, and making its way slowly toward the back of the house like some ancient crab scuttling across the floor of its cave and feeding on its own remains.

Then, as now, the bathroom was fragrant with

the scent of Palmolive soap—her favorite—and setting the flag on the toilet seat, Jesus Maria washed her hands and face with cold water and delicately patted them dry. Mama Chona had taught her daughters that washing with ice-cold water and drying gently prevented wrinkles.

She had picked up the brightly colored cloth triangle and walked into Manuel's room. Setting the flag on the bed, she lay down beside it, purposefully lying on her injured shoulder so that she might feel pain until she passed into unconsciousness. The dream she had still haunted her.

She and Manuel were dancing at a wedding in Mexico and she was enjoying feeling his arms around her. Suddenly, she found herself alone playing a piano without keys in an empty recital hall. A few moments later, she was in bare feet and dragging the piano like a cross on her right shoulder down a path strewn with thorny roses. Manuel's voice was telling her to put on her shoes and return to the dance but the blood streaming from her feet held her captive. A desert sun was beating down on her and, though very bright, its light was cold and made her tremble.

Jesus Maria awoke in darkness, shivering, with pins and needles in her legs. Dazed, she sat up and as if still in the dream, she placed the flag at the bottom of a plastic laundry basket. Methodically, she began going through Manuel's closet and clothes drawers. Unrolling his socks and emptying the pockets of old suits and trousers he had not worn in years, she found the money, a great deal of it.

Since 1929, Manuel had refused to trust any bank with his wages and she knew he had never invested money in anything except his family. Though she did not stop to count it, Jesus Maria saw that there was more than enough to pay for his funeral as well as allow her to make repairs on the house. "Oh, Manuel. You weren't such a fool, after all."

She put his clothes into the basket and carried it out to the backyard, straining her shoulder once again. The blue predawn light softened the world and she could just make out the outline of the mountain to the northeast. The stillness of the early desert morning was her only witness as she carefully and dutifully burned the garments, one by one. She felt like a high priestess performing an ancient ritual.

When Serena came to take her to mass, Jesus Maria was ready and waiting on the front porch swing. "Good morning," she said to her niece.

"My God, Tia, have you been up all night?"

"No, my dear Serena. I got up earlier than usual to ask forgiveness for my sins." The smoke was still in her throat and eyes and she kept having to pat her face with a white lace handkerchief that had belonged to Mama Chona.

"Are you catching a cold, Tia?"

"No, no, my child. It's just the dust from this desert that always bothers me. You know that."

...
xiii

"It's been nine months," Jesus Maria said to her grieving self and left Manuel's room. The coldness of the air in the back porch made her crave another cup of coffee.

Jesus Maria almost never drank it after noon, but in honor of the holiday and because she was feeling a strangeness seeping in through the pain in her shoulder, she made up her mind to stay up late and watch the Christmas programs on television. Every Christmas Eve since he bought their first set in the early fifties, she had criticized Manuel for doing exactly that instead of accompanying her to church. From the kitchen, Jesus Maria sensed that Manuel was waiting for her in the parlor and the back of her neck became very warm. Stirring slowly, she watched the granules of instant coffee dissolve.

Manuel had waited for her in that same silent and patient way throughout their courtship. When she first saw him at the Esmeralda Drugstore on Second Street, Jesus Maria thought him the handsomest man in the world. His wavy, black hair was wet and he looked like a dark terracotta angel freshly emerged from the southside canal. He offered her his place in the checkout line.

"Are you from Zacatecas?" she asked before thanking him.

"No," he said and that was all.

"Well, you should be. All the people from there have skin just like yours." His embarrassment thrilled her.

"My name is Manuel Chavez," he said softly. "I'm from Jalisco."

She shook his hand like an American and embarrassed him even more. Jesus Maria thanked him and left the store without telling him her name. For a week, from the second-story window of Tia Cuca's apartment, she watched him enter the Esmeralda at the hour of their meeting and wondered what she would do.

"Invite him to come here for coffee," Tia Cuca told her. "I'm tired of seeing your moon face at that window. I promise I won't tell your mother."

"Oh, bless you, Tia," she said. Coffee was a forbidden luxury in Mama Chona's house. She called it "the Devil's brew."

Smelling it on her breath after her first meeting with Manuel, Mama Chona had looked at her and said, "Jesus Maria, as the oldest child in this family, you must continue with your schooling so that you can get a good job and help support your younger brothers and sisters. You are a very intelligent girl, daughter, and very strong. I want the best for you. Had my dearest first child lived, I would not ask this sacrifice of you. You must be strong and not marry for a while." Her last child—also called Miguel—was not yet ten years old.

"*Si*, Mamá. I promise," Jesus Maria said. After the second meeting with him, Jesus Maria gargled Tía Cuca's cologne.

"What's that lavender smell?" Mama Chona asked her. "It's strange. There's coffee in it."

On their third meeting in secret, the small and bright yellow chrysanthemums Manuel gave her fed her hungry heart. When he left, her aunt said, "I wonder if that poor boy got those flowers from the cemetery. You know, Jesus Maria, the heart is happy with crumbs. I think you are in love with love and not with that handsome young man."

"I don't know what you are talking about, Tia. I enjoy drinking coffee with him." Jesus Maria believed her own lies and fell in love without a struggle. In all innocence, she did not mention their rendezvous to her confessor.

A year later and a week after the high school commencement ceremony, she married him without her mother's permission. At the end of the small reception at Tia Cuca's, Mama Chona embraced her daughter and said, "God be with you, Jesus Maria. You're going to need Him." From that moment, she had watched her life become a vale of tears and regrets, and not once had Mama Chona extended her beautiful hand in pity or solace.

She added powdered milk and three lumps of sugar to the coffee and sat at the table with the ghost of her mother. "Oh, Mamá, I miss our arguments. How in the world did you survive in this desert without love?" Jesus Maria sipped from the mug.

Traveling by cart and carriage in the dark through the wastelands of Chihuahua, Mama Chona had given birth to her last child, Miguel Grande. The older children, accompanied by neighbors and servants, had followed. Mama Chona, about to deliver, was taken ahead by their father and they would not know until weeks later, when they miraculously found themselves alive in Juarez, that Jesus Angel was dead and that Mama Chona had delivered.

Left behind by their parents, Jesus Maria, her sisters Eduviges and Mema, her brothers Armando and Felix slept in terror under beds and in wardrobe cabinets during the day and heard the guns outside killing masters and servants alike. One morning, Jesus Maria and her sisters crawled to the window of the abandoned house where they were hiding until nightfall and watched the early light touch the corpses of men, women, and children scattered like straw on the street below.

"What's the matter with them?" Mema asked. She was the youngest sister.

"They're dead," Eduviges said.

"What's that?"

"It's when your soul leaves your body and doesn't come back," Jesus Maria said. "Be quiet or we'll get into trouble."

The light reached an Indian woman holding an

infant. She had fallen backward in a sitting position against the adobe wall of a house across from them. They were as still as the morning air. Mema began to cry. In the distance, a cock crowed triumphantly.

"I'm never, ever coming back to this country again," Jesus Maria said.

"You are not out of it yet," Ignacio Calderon said. He wrenched them from their perch and scolded them. His furious whispers were terrifying. In tears, Mema and Eduviges ate the crusts of bread he offered them. Jesus Maria asked about their brothers and was told to be quiet. Tenderly, Ignacio's wife, Socorro, hid them throughout the house so that they might rest for the next night's journey through the crimson wastes of their homeland.

Alone and awake under a covered bench in the kitchen, Jesus Maria licked the dirt floor in hunger and tasted the limestone. "It's good for you," she heard Mama Chona say. "It keeps your teeth strong and healthy."

"Our teeth and our souls," Jesus Maria said and put another lump of sugar in her coffee. "The truth is I cannot save my own soul any more than I can bite my own teeth." Her mother's ghost smiled across the table. Jesus Maria smiled back and walked out of the kitchen in terror.

She had felt that same fear when Mama Chona told her about Jesus Angel's death. Her father was not supposed to die and leave them stranded on the border.

"We were in the same room, Jesus Maria. I was so ashamed. The wounded and dying were all around us and blood was everywhere. The smell was revolting. 'Jesus, Jesus,' I called out to him. 'Forgive me.' He could barely speak and every breath was agony for him. He had been struck by the train that brought us to Juarez. Oh God, I can still see him helping the people forced onto the tracks by the mob. The noise was unbearable.

"The first labor pain came when I saw him sprawled out on the ground. I went to him as fast as I could. I did not want him to suffer. Please let him be dead, I prayed. But he wasn't. When he looked at me with those clear eyes, I fainted.

"He lived for as long as it took me to give birth to your brother. In the first hours of labor, he said my name over and over, 'Chona, Chona.' He could not see me on the cot next to his and I could not move to touch him. 'I'm here, Jesus, I'm here.' I don't know if he heard me.

"I am going to tell you a secret, *mija,* which you must never repeat to anyone, not even your brothers and sisters. Your oldest brother was my heart, Jesus Maria. But your father was my reason to go on living after I no longer cared to draw another breath, God forgive me. Without him, my life has no meaning and I will have nothing to offer Jesus and His Holy Mother at the hour of my death.

"I felt myself dissolving into a thousand pieces and melting into the mystery of the universe. I saw the baby's head. I was straining and pushing so that it would be out of me quickly. I wanted to comfort your father. My pain was giving me life. His pain was taking it away. Oh, *mija,* never, ever love another human being that much.

"Jesus stopped breathing the moment he heard your brother's first cry into the world. Only seconds before, he said, 'It goes on, Chona. It goes on.' He meant life, I'm certain of it."

But the way her mother had repeated Jesus Angel's last words was not at all certain. She sensed that Mama Chona was keeping something essential to herself, but Jesus Maria was too overwhelmed by the pain and horror of these revelations to ask what that was. Also, she did not understand why her mother had chosen her to hear this tale of woe and loss.

"Promise me that you will never tell anyone. I do not want the world to know how your father died."

Jesus Maria promised. At the time, it did not occur to her to wonder why Mama Chona was so insistent. Let the world believe that Jesus Angel had been assumed into heaven. After several years, even she began believing that he had been.

She remembered, too, the comical look in Mama Chona's eyes that awful first month of wandering up and down the border town's main street when, handing her infant son to Jesus Maria outside yet one more door where aid and comfort might be found, Mama Chona had said so that only she could hear, "Perhaps I'll sell him. Nothing in this life is ever ours, anyway." Those words and that look had shocked Jesus Maria into seeing the world through her mother's eyes once again.

She walked toward the parlor, watching carefully for any folds or suspicious lumps in the dining room rug. She turned on the television set and, slowly pushing the hassock in front of Manuel's easy chair, made herself comfortable. Ordinarily, true to her Carmelite upbringing, Jesus Maria scorned comfort and sat halfway into a chair, back straight and small feet flat on the floor ready to fly into action against any demon foolish enough to enter her home. She had no defenses against the ghosts of her mother and husband. Shutting her eyes, she leaned deeply into the chair and put up her feet.

For a few moments, she thought about the half-empty bottle of brandy hidden behind the novels on the top shelf of the dining room bookcase, but her shoulder was beginning to bother her and she was too comfortable to get up from Manuel's chair. She raised the mug toward the ceiling in a toast to no one in particular.

The light in the house was an eerie, amber color that warmed and puzzled her. "How can this be? The sun went down hours ago." She half expected Manuel to tell her that it came back up just to annoy her. In a voice filled with emotion, she called out his name into the light and then chided herself for being so silly and stupid.

The program vibrating in front of her brought her back to earth. It was a country-western celebration of the birth of Christ and an especially friendly woman with a huge bosom and wearing an enormous blond wig was talking to her. Enthralled, Jesus Maria was glad no one was there to see her so amused by such appalling behavior. She decided to have a taste of the brandy after all when the blond woman started singing a song about Santa's reindeer transporting the baby Jesus all over the world and spreading love like butter. Her voice made Jesus Maria feel very jolly.

The amber light disappeared and only the smell of the brandy as she poured a capful into the coffee made her feel Manuel's presence. He was standing behind her in that place on the carpet where they had fallen together.

"It's true," she said, keeping her eyes on the rug. "Nothing ever dies. Oh, God in heaven, then why am I so afraid?"

She believed in Jesus and His resurrection. Why not in her own? Wasn't that what her entire life had been devoted to reaching? Why was Manuel's ghost and the light, now brighter than before, frightening her so? Out of the past, she heard him propose.

"Come with me, Jesus Maria. Leave your mother. You and I, we will make life out of nothing at all."

The brandy scalded her throat. "Stay where you are," she said through her coughing. "Don't come back. You've suffered enough."

She walked into and out of the light, her heart beating wildly against her shoulder. When she reached his chair, the coughs subsided. She sat down on the hassock and took two long swallows from the mug. This time, the smoky flavor of the cognac calmed her.

After a while, she thought she heard a knock at the door. Jesus Maria wanted to believe it came from the program she was watching until she could no longer ignore the rapping sounds at the front-door window.

The remote-control switch Manuel had taught her to use was nowhere in sight and her arm was bothering her too much to turn off the set. She looked toward the dining room and kitchen to make certain all ghosts had vanished. Before opening the door, she drank the rest of the lukewarm coffee and did not care that her breath smelled of bitter apples.

xiv

Miguel Grande, Juanita, and Miguel Chico were on her front porch. Before Jesus Maria unlatched the screen door, her brother said in a loud voice, "What are you doing, sister? Waiting for Manuel to pay you a visit?"

"Yes," Jesus Maria said as brashly. "What's it to

you?" She embraced him and smelled the cigarette smoke that clung to his clothes like a shield.

"*Feliz navidad, comadre,*" she said to Juanita. "And Mickie, how are you? I haven't seen you in such a long time. You young people forget about us oldies."

"I'm here now, Tia." He hugged her. By then, his aunt was unable to lift her arm and they pretended not to notice.

Before Jesus Maria could turn off the television, Miguel Chico said, "No, please, don't. I like that woman a lot."

"She sure has big tits," Miguel Grande said.

"Oh, shut up, Miguel, Mr. One-track-mind. And how are you, *comadre?* I hope your arm isn't bothering you too much. We all missed you at Santa Lucia and decided to leave the party at Alicia's early to come and see you. Everyone asked about you and sends greetings." Juanita was generous with her fibs and saw that her sister-in-law was not taken in by them.

"Well, you know, *comadre,* I feel myself to be so old and this worthless arm is killing me. Anyway, I couldn't think of celebrating without Manuel here." She pointed toward his chair and they turned to look. Miguel Chico was surprised his uncle did not materialize before them. It was clear that he was alive in Jesus Maria's eyes. Miguel Grande broke the spell by sitting in Manuel's chair.

"Can I get you something warm to drink?" his aunt asked.

"No, *comadre,*" Juanita said. "We stopped by to

see if you wanted to go for a little ride around town."

"In this frost? Never, *comadre.*" She wiped her eyes. Her cheekbones glowed.

Jesus Maria seemed so pure to Miguel Chico, so innocent about the world, despite the anger in her voice when she complained about the imperfections of her life. Earlier that evening, he had said to Josie that Jesus Maria was the true nun in the family.

"She's hard and innocent, sweet and tough as nails." Josie laughed at him.

"Oh, cousin," she said. "You are so romantic about women. Jesus Maria is anything but a nun."

Instead of watching the blond woman on the set, Miguel Chico was looking at his aunt and imagining her in a habit, wearing one of those white starched headdresses that made him see herons on the wing.

"What are you grinning about, devil?" Jesus Maria asked him with affection.

"At what's going on in this program," he said. Only her constantly watering eyes made him think that Jesus Maria was "the old lady" she kept telling them she was.

The country-western star was now strumming a guitar and singing a Christmas song for all the children in the audience and the world. She was surrounded by dwarfs in colorful and bizarre costumes, and Miguel Chico fought hard to keep from laughing hysterically.

"Isn't she curious?" Jesus Maria asked them, her eyes twinkling. "She's like a female Liberace." They laughed. Miguel Chico saw himself as a child kissing her cheek and laying his head in her lap.

Miguel Grande blew his nose and put out a second cigarette. "Come on, sister," he said. "Let's go see all the Christmas lights. We'll drive around the rich people's part of town and see how much money they're giving the electric company this year."

He spoke to Jesus Maria with humor and affection. Since Mama Chona's death, Miguel Grande had begun to see her as more than a religious fanatic.

"You haven't taken a ride in my new car. Manuel helped me pick it out just before you got out of the hospital." He rose slowly out of the chair. The cold was affecting his knees. He called the '74 Chevy his "Mexican Cadillac."

"Oh, no. I couldn't possibly go anywhere," Jesus Maria said and touched her arm gently as if testing it. "It's much too cold and I'm afraid to expose this useless limb to any more abuse. Please, you go on without me. Don't feel you have to stay any longer with this invalid good-for-nothing."

"We won't take no for an answer, especially from an invalid," Juanita said. She had prepared her husband and son for Jesus Maria's refusal.

"Mickie, go and find this *viejita*'s coat, the winter one, and make sure the back door is locked. Miguel, get going. Start warming up the car."

Juanita was able to approach Jesus Maria in ways the rest of the family did not dare. Three years earlier, she had urged her sister-in-law to celebrate her fiftieth wedding anniversary with a mass in the Cathedral and a reception at the Daughters of Mary Hall.

"Ay, no, *comadre*, please," Jesus Maria had cried into the phone. "Promise me that you will not even mention that you asked this of me."

"It's because you don't want anyone to guess your age, isn't it, *comadre?* Who cares? We'll have a wonderful time and we can have all the usual arguments and pretend that you had Gaspar when you were ten years old. We'll dance and dance and dance! I'll help you with all that needs to be done."

"No, no, *comadre*," Jesus Maria said, terrified. At the end of the conversation, she used the common Angel family ploy of getting others to obey them by saying, "If you love me, you won't do this." Juanita obeyed.

She helped Jesus Maria put on her dark brown winter coat. "No, please, in God's name. Look out for my arm," she said and moved in ways that told Juanita she was willing to be kidnapped.

"Don't worry, Tia," Miguel Chico said in a tone of conspiracy. "It's still early. After our drive, we can stop at my parents' house for a little glass of something to warm us up." He had noticed the brandy bottle on the shelf with the novels he had read in his childhood and adolescence. "I promise to bring you back whenever you want, but only after you spend some time with us."

He was anxious to leave his aunt's house. From

239

the first, its otherworldliness made him ill at ease.

"All right," Jesus Maria said to him in a flirtatious way. "But, you promise. Only for a short time. I'm still in mourning."

"Yes, Tia, I know. But it's Christmas. Surely God will forgive you."

Juanita gave him a sharp look. "Come on, now. Mickie, take your aunt's arm. Be careful, both of you. It's very slippery." She walked ahead of them. "I love Christmas Eve!"

They stepped into the icy night. The mountain was white with frost and the sky was a dark gray lit from an unknown source. Miguel Chico wondered if there were a full moon above it and became instantly melancholy.

In the backseat with him, Jesus Maria feit the shift in his mood. Before her, the lights of the on-coming cars turned her brother's head into a flashing silhouette. No one spoke and the whirring of the car heater made her very sleepy.

As his father drove into a neighborhood on the northwest side of town, Miguel Chico was thinking how much he did not love Christmas Eve. To escape from his thoughts, he looked out of the window.

The homes on both sides of the street had been built in the late sixties and early seventies. Large and expensive-looking, they perched on rolling desert hills at the foot of the highest peak in the range. Most of them were brick dwellings in a mix of styles that made him and his cousins laugh. "Southwest

American Colonial," Josie called it. "I'd rather live in a teepee."

Tended and designed by Mexican gardeners, the landscaping had flourished and softened the sharpness of the brick. Lawns, faded dirty blond by the winter, were wide and spacious. Some of the trees and shrubs, evergreen and deciduous, had grown quite large. In their midst, ocotillo, yucca, and century plants were artfully placed and reminded Miguel Chico that he was in the desert.

"Tell us again where we are, Tia Jesus Maria," they loved asking as children.

"We are at the bottom of what was once a prehistoric sea. Every day, they find fossils of ancient marine creatures at the very top of these mountains. Isn't it amazing what God can do?"

"But why did He turn it into a desert?"

"So that we could live in the sky. The clouds are our fish. Look how many different kinds there are."

The streets became a carnival of brightly colored lights when Miguel Grande drove toward the mountain. Blue, white, red, and green flashed into the night. Nativity scenes, Santa Clauses, and their reindeer, altar boy choirs and *luminarios* were expertly set up on walks and lawns, roofs and porches. Theirs was one of many cars driving slowly by these Christmas offerings.

"How beautiful!" Jesus Maria said. She was genuinely impressed. "Don't you think it's beautiful, Mickie?"

They were passing by a gigantic Christmas tree made entirely of tumbleweeds spray-painted white and lit from within by a light that shifted from color to color. Astonished, Jesus Maria was seeing the color and shape of the world emerge from the grayness of the last months of mourning.

"Yes," Miguel Chico answered her from a hollow place inside his chest.

"What's wrong? What's the matter?" She spoke in a whisper, barely able to make out his face in profile.

Above the noise of the heater, Miguel Chico heard his parents' joyful exclamations. Their voices were unreal in his ears and he was seeing them as unfamiliar shades in a journey he had begun into an unknown and forbidden land. Jesus Maria's words came to him from the lifeless figures on the lawns and roofs outside, delayed by the coldness of the night.

"What's wrong?" they asked him in her voice. He did not answer.

Jesus Maria looked at him closely once again. "Why, Mickie, you are crying."

"No, Tia, I just have something in my contact lenses and it's making my eyes water. It happens all the time in the desert. I'll be all right in a minute."

Jesus Maria held her tongue and looked out on the holiday scene. Miguel Grande had stopped in front of an enormous desert willow. Each of its delicate, bare branches had been strung with the small, clear Christmas lights that made Jesus Maria think of the fireflies she had seen on the journey north from Mexico. When she asked her about them, Mama Chona had called them the spirits of newly made angels.

In a light breeze, the frosted limbs of the tree were swaying like magic wands, at once beckoning and comforting. The night above them was intensely white.

Miguel Chico's throat began to ache. Who are these strangers? What are they celebrating? Who is this God? He could not feel himself breathe or hear the beating of his heart.

A few years before, in a third and unexpected operation, he had been given a spinal anesthetic. The table was slanted so that his head was below his feet, forcing him to look up once more into the arctic lighting he had grown to detest. He was told that when the medication reached his chest, he would not be able to feel himself breathe and that he need not be afraid.

A pleasant numbing began in his toes and crept dreamily and methodically from muscle to muscle, joint to joint, like hundreds of razor blades chopping up his nervous system. When it embraced his ribs, Miguel Chico became panic-stricken and begged with his eyes to be put under completely.

Sitting beside his aunt, Miguel Chico was kept by that same numbness from bolting out of the car and away from his life, driven by a desire to be anywhere except in this world. His eyes saw nothing.

Jesus Maria sensed his soul in torment. Her nephew's face, reflecting the light from the tree, was colorless. The branches of the desert willow called to them. In a matter-of-fact tone, Jesus Maria broke into the silence. "You know, it was very inconsiderate of Manuel to die on me without a word of warning."

Miguel Chico laughed, too loudly at first, then more naturally as his father drove them home. He ran into the den and restored his balance with two quick swallows of whiskey.

Shortly before midnight, he drove his aunt home. After unlocking the front door, he handed her the keys. A small plastic figure of the Sacred Heart of Jesus hung on the chain. He faced her.

Jesus Maria was looking at him with watery eyes. Raising her good arm, she touched his face tenderly. The brown velvet of her glove almost broke his resolve to be without feeling for the rest of his life. Letting go in love was too difficult for him.

"Mickie, I want you to remember what I'm going to tell you," she said in the Angel manner of imparting wisdom by mocking it. She looked at him without pity.

"God squeezes our throats occasionally, but He does not strangle us."

Bending him toward her lovely face, Jesus Maria kissed his cheek. She smelled of soap and smoke and he felt they were at the bottom of a dry, dry sea.

"Feliz navidad," she said. "And God bless you, Mickie, even if you don't believe. Come and see me before you go back to California."

He promised he would. "And I'll tell Josie and the girls what you said about God."

"Yes, do that. Be careful on the walk." She watched him hurry away into the dark and went into her house.

"Manuel?" she called. "Are you there?"

XV

In his room at Santa Lucia, Gabriel moved from the bed to the window and back on the bare wood floor. The house smelled of Doña Marina's tamales and red *chile,* and he offered up the urge to sneak into the kitchen for a midnight snack. The flavors of Alicia's feast were still in his mouth.

Shutting the blinds, he saw the frost forming on the panes. He felt the cold through his blue slippers and robe and held his arms close to his body as he walked back and forth.

He prayed for all the Angels, beginning with the youngest and ending with his mother and father and brothers. He prayed for Doña Marina and Manitas and for the special intentions of his parishioners. He did not forget *la señora* Olguin and her committee and threw in the county sheriff and His Eminence the Bishop for good measure.

"Let Josie find a husband and please heal Jesus Maria's arm. Allow joy to enter my brother Miguel Chico's life and may the Church accept people like him with love. We are all your children. Help my father to stop smoking and my mother to stop worrying. May aunts Eduviges and Mema be cured of their arthritis and keep Serena in good health to care for us all."

He prayed for the altar boys and the gang members, for the sick and the dead and the dying in and out of his parish, for the poor and hungry, the rich and privileged. "May we all be comforted by the miracle of the Nativity every day of our lives."

Breathing into his hands, he prayed for all souls in torment and in purgatory. In particular, he asked that the souls of Mama Chona, his uncles Felix, Armando, and Manuel be remembered.

While putting the robe at the foot of the bed and the slippers under it to warm them through the night, Gabriel prayed for his own soul. He thanked God for his fears and doubts and asked for the strength to struggle with them. He felt closest to God in his weakness. At last, he got under the covers and after several long yawns, Gabriel prayed for the reign of peace and good will to begin.

His heart was filled with pity and gratitude. In the moments before sleep, Manitas appeared like an angel at the foot of the bed.

"What are you doing here, Manitas?"

"Get up. We have something to do," the old man said.

"Not now. It's very late and I'm tired. Can't it wait?"

"No, *padrecito,* it can't wait." Manitas whispered nonsense words into his ear and in an instant they were standing outside the gymnasium door under a bright desert sun.

"Andale, do it," Manitas told him.

"Are you sure?"

Without another word, Manitas watched Gabriel unchain the statue and free it from its cage. The wrought-iron grating melted away and the maiden's eyes flew into her face. She floated toward them and asked Gabriel to dance.

"I don't know how," he said.

Manitas was laughing and laughing.

"I'll show you," she said.

AVON ▲ TRADE
PAPERBACKS